ALSO BY EMILY GOLUS

Escape to Vindor

Mists of Paracosmia

A CLASSIC RETOLD SERIES

Break the Beast - Allison Tebo

Crack the Stone - Emily Golus

Steal the Morrow - Jenelle Leanne Schmidt

Unearth the Tides - Alissa J. Zavalianos

Raise the Dead - Nina Clare

Summon the Light - Tor Thibeaux

Chase the Legend - Hannah Kaye

Kill the Dawn - Emily Hayse

Riddle of Hearts - Rosie Grymm

Learn more at AClassicRetold.com

WORLD OF VINDOR

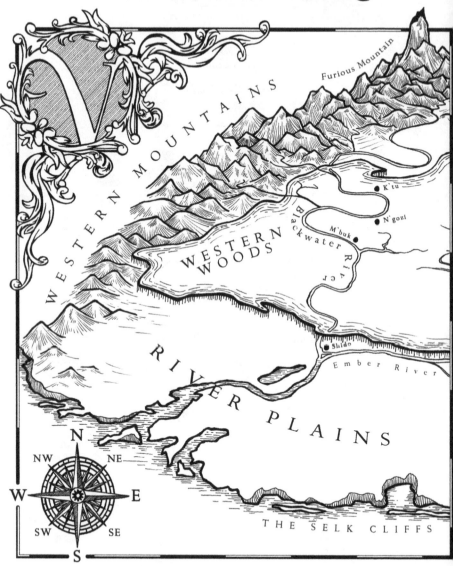

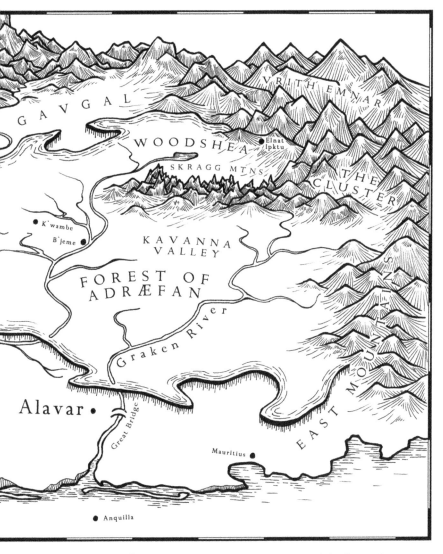

Explore the interactive map at WorldofVindor.com

A CLASSIC RETOLD

CRACK THE STONE

EMILY GOLUS

First paperback edition September 2023.

Book Design by MiblArt (www.miblart.com)

Map Design by Michael Golus

ISBN 979-8-218-21472-2

www.EmilyGolusBooks.com

AClassicRetold.com

CONTENTS

To my sons, David Bryson and Jonathan Arden.
I love you all the days ever.

"The pupil dilates in darkness and in the end finds light."

—Victor Hugo, *Les Misérables*

1

VALSHARA

On day three, the coal-black tunnel drove me into a wall of rock—a dead end in total darkness.

Scraping my claws blindly against the unyielding stone, I found a crack in the surface. My fingers traced it to an opening about ten inches tall, and I crammed myself into it.

My claws scratched at the limestone, pulling my emaciated body forward inch by inch. The rough stone bit into my bare scalp, my elbows, and anything else not protected by my ragged prison uniform.

The space was so tight that taking a full breath was impossible. Good—that would help me conserve air.

After an hour of scrabbling in utter darkness, I wondered if this had been a mistake.

My first wrong turn had probably been when I'd left the underground stream for a narrow side tunnel. I should have stayed the course, followed the broad path lit by the faint blue glow of cave moss. But that way had seemed too obvious, too open. Paranoia took over, driving me towards smaller and darker passages.

Should I turn back?

I shuddered. The thought of losing ground and returning to my old trail made me ill. He might be waiting there.

Actually, he could be following me now.

My arms flailed forward, forcing my body into the ever-narrowing crack. I turned my head sideways to avoid scraping my face on the cave floor.

The iron shackle on my wrist hit the limestone with a heart-stopping *clang*.

For a terrible second, my world froze.

Finally, I stretched out my other hand—the unshackled one—and tried to pull myself forward.

Nothing. My head was wedged in too tight. I'd reached the bitter end.

I had three options.

One: retrace my path and risk my pursuer intercepting me.

Two: use my light and risk him seeing me.

Three: surrender and die here.

At least in the third scenario I'd remain free. I curled up my small, green body as much as I could in the dark crack. As a final farewell, I whispered my well-practiced litany of curses, calling down misery on the wardens, the Guidelights, and everyone who'd wronged me.

No. Heat rose up inside me. *I am Valshara, the black stone born of fire. Break me, and my edges turn into knives.*

I will live.

Inhaling, I tasted the stale air. The narrow space smelled of something other than just limestone—I caught a slight whiff of decay.

I clicked my tongue, wincing at the risky disruption in the silence. But it confirmed what I had noticed before—this narrow fissure didn't echo properly.

Shifting my position, I ran my hands against the stone above me. Something soft tickled my skin.

My body tensed. I needed light. If I didn't know what I was dealing with, I wouldn't make it out alive.

Stretching out my clawed fingers, I willed them to glow.

Instead of the natural yellowish-green light that goblins are born with, my fingertips shone blood-red.

When the tattooist had injected the red pigment into my fingers dot by dot, I'd seen it as a mark of savage pride—a triumph for me, the first female to make the ranks. I never dreamed it would make me an easy target.

In the dim red light, tiny white threads hung from the stone.

My heart skipped a beat. Not threads—roots.

Roots meant plants. Plants meant the Topside world was just above me. A few feet and I'd be free of the cavern system entirely.

I dug my ragged claws into the crackled limestone ceiling and pulled.

Of course, there was a good chance that doing so would cause a cave-in, killing me instantly. Or worse, trapping me until I suffocated or starved. But that kind of death—any death really—would be better than going back to the Pit.

Pebbles and dust fell into my face and I suppressed the urge to cough. I worked desperately for five, maybe ten minutes, digging upward into powdery soil.

Something flashed through the hole above.

Light.

I clawed my way through with renewed energy. The dot of flickering yellow light grew above me.

A moment later, sunlight—horrible, burning, wonderful sunlight—poured into the shaft. I thrust my body through the opening and into the open air.

The shifting yellow light seared my retinas. I scrambled away from my hole in the earth, half-expecting a hand to grab my ankle then and there.

Fibers wrapped around my arms and legs. I panicked, ripping a set of roots out of the earth.

My vision was nearly useless in this blazing light, but I recognized the silhouette of a leaf. These plants were huge and stringy with broad fronds—nothing like the mosses and lichens native to my world.

They also provided a decent amount of cover. I crouched beneath a patch of leaves, waiting for my vision to adjust so I could make a run for it without hurting myself.

My fingers reached into my tattered uniform and drew out my shiv. I tested the black edge of the weapon with a calloused finger and drew blood.

I'd discovered this shard of *valshara*—black obsidian, my namesake—while crushing ore in the Pit mine. While the wardens weren't watching, I'd chiseled it with a rock, the glassy stone yielding razor-sharp edges.

I had fantasized about killing anything—or better yet, anyone —that got in the way of my escape. Now was the time.

Peering around the green leaf, I squinted at the flickering light on the horizon. Beside it blazed a second light.

I'd only been above ground once during my military training, but I knew that it didn't have two suns.

I turned. Three more yellow lights burned, hovering above stone urns. Above me, stalactites dangled from a solid stone ceiling.

This wasn't the Topside world at all. Somehow I was still underground.

In the grey soil beneath my clawed feet, stems and leaves rose from the ground in neat rows. Only one species favored unnaturally straight lines like this. There was an awful smell, too—not just of soil, but something sour with a bit of spice and—

Thump. Something heavy landed on top of me and tangled around my limbs. Coils of fiber—a net.

Before I could react, the ropes constricted around me.

I thrashed my limbs to no avail. Three gangly creatures wrestled the net closed, cinching it with a heavy cord. Then they backed away, gawking at me with their grotesque faces.

Humans.

They were ugly creatures—nearly twice my height, with eyes

comically small for their faces and ears that were stubby and round. Their skin—at least what wasn't covered up by layers of white clothing—was about as dark as my own, but reddish-brown instead of green. Ghastly white strings sprouted from their heads, and one of them actually had the stuff growing out of his face, under his bulbous nose.

But their looks were nothing compared to their *stench*. When humans overheat, they secrete a stinking liquid from their skin. These humans had apparently gotten quite warm wrestling me into the net.

My eyes watered.

If I hadn't been so distracted by the mystery of the lights—which I could now tell were just urns of yellow flame—I'd have smelled them sooner and stabbed them all.

I didn't care if they were only fieldworkers, startled by a goblin digging through their crops. I'd have still killed them without remorse.

The net was too heavy for me to wrestle my way out of, and a scrap of broken metal on my shackle had gotten entangled in the fibers. My shiv might be able to saw through the rope, but it would take some time.

I snarled at the humans. "You mans." I racked my brain for the little bit of Vindorian I'd learned at the military academy. The emphasis had been on eavesdropping on Topside enemies, not on speaking, but a bit of threatening couldn't be too hard.

"You come here me, I shiv you. I crack you like stones. I bash in you toes."

I was fairly sure that last word was the term for "skulls" in Vindorian. Whatever exactly I said, the humans stepped further back.

I drew my shiv and tried to saw the rope as subtly as I could. But I hadn't gotten far when five more humans appeared, each holding a torch of silver fire. The largest man carried some sort of club.

Guards. My blood went cold.

The big guard chatted with the fieldworkers for a moment, then approached the net, looming over me. I braced myself.

"Well, this is unexpected." The guard spoke in crystal-clear Goblin.

What?

He continued. "I assume you have escaped from the Masters?"

How could this human speak our language, and know about the Dominion's ruling political party? Perhaps I was in more danger than I'd estimated. If these humans somehow had dealings with the Masters, or even an agreement with them—

My vision went black around the edges.

"Do you understand?" the big guard asked. "Did you—"

"Please," I heard myself whimpering. "Don't take me back."

The big guard nodded to his companions, and the world lurched as they lifted the net with me inside.

The big guard drew closer, his small brown eyes looking into mine. "There are others here like you. Others who have escaped."

"What?"

"We will take you to them. But we will leave you bound because the farmers said you threatened them. The goblins of Ipktu can decide your worthiness."

2

BLOOD HAND

I pktu. Surely the big guard had misspoken. Ipktu wasn't a real place—it was a setting for children's tales.

And ... others who had escaped the Pit? The wardens were ruthless. Surely they hadn't lost track of multiple prisoners.

Of course, the wardens weren't finely trained hunters. It was only when a Blood Hand went missing that the Faceless arose.

I shuddered.

Outside of the heavy net, the underground human city passed by, with its clean stone walls, brightly colored lights, and masses of stinking humans. I worked my blade, but sawing the ropes while bouncing along proved to be more difficult than I'd anticipated.

The guards took me down a flight of stairs once or twice, until they came to a much darker level of the city. My aching eyes relaxed.

At last the humans stopped and lowered the net to the lime-stone floor.

They were releasing me. I gripped the shiv in my fingers.

But before the guards opened the mouth of the net—before I sprang upon them to attack—I heard skittering sounds behind broken walls and rows of stalagmites, and detected an all-too-familiar smell.

We were completely surrounded by goblins.

I tucked my shiv back into my tattered pocket and stood motionless as the net fell away around me.

"We found this one on a Level Four farm," the big guard announced to the unseen goblins. "He seems to have stumbled into us by mistake."

"She," a soft goblin voice corrected.

"Oh, yes. She," the big guard said. "No offense meant, Queen Nara—I have a hard time telling."

"None taken," the soft-voiced goblin answered. She stepped into the silvery light of the human torches and regarded me for a moment.

I sneered. This "queen" was a Lowblood.

"We'll leave you to your business, then." The group of guards retreated with their torches, leaving me and the Lowblood in welcome darkness.

More goblins stepped out into the open, surrounding me on all sides. I tensed. A few were missing fingers or the points to their ears, and most of them had glossy scars on their dark green skin—particularly on their wrists where shackles once had been.

There were probably fifty of them. Who were these people?

A young male approached me, holding up his clawed hand in the traditional greeting. "We see the way," he said, his fingers glowing a soft yellow-green.

I froze.

Suspicious murmurs broke out all around.

I raised my trembling fingers. "We see the way," I said, and willed my fingers to glow. They shone bright red.

"Blood Hand, Blood Hand!" the crowd screeched.

Before I could reach my shiv, several goblins shoved me to the floor and piled on top of me, striking me with their fists.

"You dragged my mother to the Pit, you monster."

"Thought you could come to take us back?"

I writhed under the crush of bodies but couldn't get free. I gasped for air.

"Stop! What is this meaning?"

At the sound of the new voice, the goblins shrank away. I coughed, struggling to rise, and glanced up at the new figure before me.

He was small and crouched over in an odd way, but the other goblins bowed their heads as though he were a mighty leader.

"She's a Blood Hand," one of the others explained. "The Masters' secret police. Her kind are cruel, forcing innocent goblins to—"

"I've heared of Blood Hands," the leader said. "But they maked no more trouble, I thinked."

The gnarled figure, the barely understandable grammar—it couldn't be. These Ipktu goblins were fawning over a Slasher. The lowest of Lowbloods, uneducated, no more than a fighting dog.

And yet here he was, a revered leader. What kind of upside-down place was this?

"Yes," said one of the other goblins. "The Blood Hands were removed from power in the Traitors' Rebellion."

"When the Guidelights took the Masters' capital, and then brokered deals instead of bringing justice—"

Several goblins growled, and one spat on the ground.

"—they sentenced all Blood Hands to the Pit. That was six years ago."

Six years—that was even longer than I'd counted. My blood boiled.

The Slasher leader held out his hand to me. I scowled and turned my face away. He had no right to look someone of my rank in the eye.

Undeterred, the Slasher brushed his fingers against my wrist shackle. "It's an olden-style iron, yes? Very heavy. Always biting because it's too tightened." He glanced back at the crowd of goblins. "How many of Ipktu knowed this hurt."

"It's not the same," a Highblood goblin insisted.

"Why different?" The Slasher leader rose. "Did she suffer less hardly because she is Blood Hand? Is she wanting freedom any less than you wanted?"

No one answered.

"And she's runned away here, wanting the same all you have. I am not remembering any time we turned anyone away for what they did before the Pit. Not Slashers. Not runaway Guidelights. And now, not Blood Hands."

Silence.

The Slasher gripped my hand and pulled me to my feet. "Here in Ipktu, you are our sister. We were all slaves the same, but our chains are broken. We are all equal now, all made new."

He turned to the soft-voiced goblin. "Nara, please bring our new sister to a rest-place, and give her food. If she is injuried, call Doctor Resh. I want to talk at her, but later. She is tired and hungry and hurt."

The Lowblood "queen" gestured for me to follow her. I complied, unsure of what else to do.

The other goblins—who two minutes ago had been beating me—stepped back and let me go quietly.

Who was this Slasher with so much influence over them? And how had they gotten here, nestled within a human city?

Nara led me to a narrow hall with round doorways carved into the stone. She stopped. "This one is for you."

Pulling back a pale curtain, I found the room small and clean, with a padded blanket on the floor. I hadn't slept on anything but hard stone for six long years. I narrowed my eyes at Nara. "Who are you?"

"A former slave. I was in the Pit with my brothers, until the Bandit King rescued us."

"*Who?*"

"The Bandit King, my husband—the one you were just talking to. He's the one who brought all of us here."

The Bandit King. I'd heard that name whispered among the Pit slaves. I had assumed he was only a legend, but here he was, a real goblin—and an uneducated Slasher of all things.

"Do you need anything else?" Nara asked.

"No." I stepped into the room and crawled onto the bed. Sleep took me instantly.

3

THE BANDIT KING

I woke up with adrenaline coursing through my veins. Alone? Where were the others? I was late for roll call. I couldn't take another beating, not after I'd just been—

And I stopped. The blanket beneath me. The quiet stone room. And there, sitting by the door, a plateful of root mash.

I leapt across the room and shoved the mash into my mouth by the fistful. It was warm and unspoiled. When it was gone, I lifted the stoneware plate and licked it clean.

Then I snatched up a stone mug from the floor and gulped down water.

A set of clean linen clothes lay folded by the door. I peeled off my rags and slipped into the grey tunic and trousers, making sure to tuck the shiv into an inner pocket. A woven belt with several extra loops went around my waist, most likely designed for holding tools. These were sturdy and plain-looking clothes—the first new set I'd had in six years.

I resisted the urge to dash out of the room. There were no boulders to shove here, no frigid pits to scratch ore from. For the first time since I could remember, I could rest.

But I didn't remember how.

I paced the circumference of the small room, my mind racing.

After all of those years of pain, after the terrifying escape, suddenly I had been dropped into this quiet world where there was food and a soft bed and goblins who called me sister.

The emotion was overwhelming. It wasn't happiness—more like *lostness*.

I continued pacing.

Then there was the Bandit King.

Whenever some poor Pit slave didn't show up for roll call and was never seen again, the whisper would go through the barracks that the Bandit King had taken him in the night. I had scoffed, believing "Bandit King" was more likely a euphemism for starvation. He was a delusion of hope from those with nothing else to hope for.

Yet now I had met him, flesh and bone like me. And here was where he had been stealing all those poor souls away to.

I stopped mid-step. All those torturous years a slave, and the Bandit King had come for all sorts of Lowbloods. But never for *me*.

Heat seeped into my blood.

They'd left me behind to suffer. All of these Ipktuans had. They'd forced me to break out on my own, enduring a miserable journey in the dark. And then when I stumbled into this place by accident, they *beat* me. Just as the wardens had.

The lost feeling disappeared. Anger and hatred washed over me once again, strengthening me like a draught of firewater.

Hatred had been the force that had kept me alive all these years. I'd fought to survive out of sheer spite, to defy the wardens who'd love to see me die. At night I fantasized about reigning down terror on my captors, punishing them eye for an eye.

I felt the stone armor re-harden around my heart. How could that terrible Bandit King just *leave* me in that place?

I grabbed the stone mug and threw it against the wall. It crashed back to the floor, undamaged. I picked it back up and examined it.

And suddenly I had a plan. A way to be free of the Pit, but

also away from this settlement of Slashers and Guidelights and Lowblood dogs, far from the city of stinking humans.

And I'd be able to punish those worthless Ipktuans for what they'd done to me.

A voice from outside the curtain startled me from my thoughts.

"New-Sister, are you rested? Are you ready for me to talk at you?"

I turned. In the doorway stood the Bandit King. Alone.

A troop of bodyguards always flanked the Masters back in the Dominion, with good reason. Was the Bandit King really so naïve?

"I'm rested," I said, pretending a few hours of sleep could undo six years of sleep deprivation.

The hunched goblin pushed past the curtain into the little room. I strained my ears and sniffed as subtly as I could, but couldn't detect any other goblins nearby. Unreal.

"We have sameness, sister," he said. "For me, I was once away a time a Slasher."

"I gathered that."

"I wanted nothing but biting and tearing and slashing. But I was changed. We all in Ipktu are changed."

I nodded, mentally measuring the steps between me and the king. I inched forward.

"What is your name?"

His question took me by surprise. No one had asked that in a very long time—I'd been known only by a prisoner number. I hesitated. "Valshara Sh'a."

"Sh'a?" He scrunched his face. "You comed from Family *None*?"

"No, I came from a respectable Highblood family." I dug my claws into my palms. "But after my condemnation, my father disowned me and forbid me to speak the family name."

The Bandit King frowned. "Even if he wasn't liking you being Blood Hand, that was unkindness of him."

"Being a Blood Hand was his idea," I snarled. "He pulled the strings to get me on the force even though I was female. But when the Guidelights sent us to the Pit, he cut his ties. Didn't look good for his political career."

I swallowed back bile. *Stupid.* I'd said more than I'd meant to and the emotion threatened to dull my senses. I took a breath, readjusting my inner armor.

"You have suffered," the Bandit King said.

A hot tear started to blur my vision.

Don't lose focus, Valshara. He's a master manipulator. This must be why everyone fawns over him.

"We have many old pains in Ipktu," he said. "But here we heal. Here we have new startings for all."

He reached one hand into a pocket of his grey tunic, and with his other hand he reached for my shackle.

Now. I grabbed his outstretched arm and pulled him toward me, jerking my knee into his diaphragm. He crumpled over, gasping for breath. Then I snatched up the stone mug and smashed it into the back of his head.

He collapsed onto the blanket.

Quickly I rolled his body up in the fabric and hoisted it onto my back. I poked my head out of the doorway and, making certain the air was clear of goblin scents, fled with him down the passageway.

Immediately panic took over. Which way was the human city? Had I even paid attention to the path the guards had used to get me here? How was I going to drag this body back through the fissure in the stone?

I smelled goblins ahead as I neared the main part of the settlement. I hadn't even taken time to learn the layout of Ipktu, didn't know how to avoid crowded areas.

A groan came from the blanket on my back. He was already coming to. *No.*

I ducked behind a stand of stalagmites and unwrapped the blanket. I'd have to knock him out again.

"Why ... are you doing?" he groaned, his eyes unable to focus.

"I'm buying back my life." Where had that mug gone? I scanned the cave floor for a rock heavy enough to do the job. "When I return with the legendary Bandit King who's been stealing prisoners, the Masters will give me back my ancestral rank. No more running, no more exile, no more looking behind my shoulder."

"I know what hunts you." The Bandit King struggled to rise, his legs buckling beneath him. "This will hardly change his mind."

"Shut up." I spied the mug on the floor and lunged for it.

"Masters won't show you mercy. You will betray me and all these people, and you will suffer back in the Pit with us."

My hands shook as I raised the mug. The Bandit King raised his arms in a feeble attempt to shield himself.

But before I bashed the cup into his skull, a rough hand wrapped around my throat and flung me onto the ground.

My back hit the stone hard. Above me loomed a large Slasher, his snarl revealing white teeth filed to a point.

"It's the Blood Hand," someone shouted from behind them. "She's attacking the Bandit King."

At once the cavern pulsed with goblins, screaming and rushing at me.

I managed to roll out of the big Slasher's reach and ran, trapping myself against the wall of the cavern. I turned to find a mob blocking every possible escape.

Two more Slashers crouched at the forefront, ready to pounce on me with razor-sharp claws. Just because they were reformed didn't make them less deadly.

I straightened and set my jaw. At least these weren't prison guards—Slashers were more likely to be quick and professional, rather than drawing the process out. My escape had been brief, but at least earned me a kinder death. I braced myself.

"Stop." It was the Bandit King's voice. "You are not understanding. She is sister."

Nara rushed to him, pressing her tunic against his bleeding head. "She attacked you, love."

"No," he gasped. "She is helping me. Stop."

What?

The crush of goblins, including the Slashers, turned to him.

"What did he say?"

"She betrayed you. We saw it with our own eyes."

The injured king motioned toward his bleeding head. "I falled on a rock so hard I sawed stars in my brains. Valshara sees me and rushes after me with this blanket. She carries me to Doctor Resh."

Nara looked from the king to where I stood. "Is this true?"

My blood pounded in my ears. I couldn't speak, couldn't move.

"Is true," the king answered. "Valshara is a hero."

Nara pointed at the Slashers crouched in front of me. "Akka, Gnar. Run for Doctor Resh. We shouldn't be moving him with a head injury. Go."

And like that, my would-be executioners dashed away into the darkness.

"The rest of you," Nara said, "We need cloth for bandages, clean water, and maybe a needle."

As goblins scattered down various passages, the Bandit King motioned toward me. "Come, sister."

Somehow my frozen limbs obeyed. I moved through the thinning crowd of Ipktuans, and not one of them touched me.

As I approached, Nara bowed her head. "We misjudged you. We pride ourselves on not holding anyone's past against them, yet we assumed the worst of you. The goblins of Ipktu are ashamed. You don't deserve that kind of treatment."

My body shook—a violent trembling that started somewhere in my gut and extended to my toes and my blood-stained fingers.

"Valshara." The Bandit King reached into a pocket of his grey tunic and drew out a small iron key. A second later, the shackle on my wrist clattered to the stone floor, leaving my blistered wrist lighter than it had been in six years.

The Bandit King then picked up the stone mug and pressed it into my quivering fingers. I swore I saw a little of his blood still on the edge.

"With this cup, I steal you," he said quietly. "You no more belong to Blood Hands or the Pit. I steal you away from darkness. I buy you for light. You are new."

A moment later, other goblins pushed past me, offering Nara scraps of cloth and cups of water. I backed out of the way. When I felt I had control of my legs again, I turned my back to them.

I turned away from the Bandit King and fled.

4

DEATH OF THE PRISONER

M y calloused feet slapped against the stone floor. I picked up speed, barreling through the tunnel halls and up the stairs, navigating by impulse.

Somehow I found the brightly lit farm again, the crops still disturbed around the hole I'd dug. I ignored the protests of the fieldworkers and dropped back into the darkness.

The stone fissure took me again, squeezing my rib cage and scraping my face as I pushed back into the tiny crack—the one I'd been so desperate to escape just hours before.

I knew this black tunnel would kill me if it could. And yet I rushed back into its grip. At least it was a familiar danger.

I pushed and scraped and struggled in total darkness, slithering on my belly and forcing my way through openings barely larger than my head. The rough limestone lacerated my face and hands, but I didn't slow.

Something thudded along the damp floor behind me, the sound adding to my panic.

The stone mug. For some reason I'd looped its handle onto my belt.

I wanted to rip it off, but the tunnel was so tight I couldn't get my arm back to reach it.

A few moments later, I lay panting in a tepid puddle, exhausted. Knowing deep down running away changed nothing.

I hated him.

Or, at least, I wanted to hate him. Hatred was familiar, hatred made sense. But the Bandit King did not make sense.

I swallowed back a hot lump in my throat.

He'd welcomed me as a sister and defended me from attackers. But I'd done him no services. My own mother had never given me kindness that freely.

And how did I thank him? By assaulting him, by betraying him, by trying to force him into the same horrible fate I myself was desperate to escape.

I deserved death—swift and final. But he went out of his way to save me. To make a hero out of me.

I hated him.

Tears gathered in the corners of my eyes. I brushed them away roughly and dragged my body through the next tight pinch.

On the other side of the squeeze, the tunnel opened up. I'd made it back through the crack in the stone where I'd found my original dead end.

I stood upright for the first time in an hour, my new clothes caked with mud. But the path ahead was even more treacherous.

For the next hundred feet, the tunnel continued in a tight V of wet flowstone—dripping with water and so slick that it offered nothing to grasp onto. It had taken me nearly two hours to traverse this section on my way in, but now I rushed into it, fuming.

I hated him. It was my *right* for him to hate me back.

I braced my hands against one rock wall and my feet against the other, sliding my palms and soles along the slimy surface. Below me, broken rocks littered the bottom of the V where the two stone faces joined.

When I betrayed him, it was his duty to kill me. That's how the world worked. It was his job. But for him to absorb my hate and radiate kindness back—it was nonsense. It was immoral, it was unjust, it—

My foot slipped. For a second my body lurched downward. But I threw my arm back and caught the far wall, stopping my fall. For a moment I wobbled, my body in an awkward splayed position over the broken rocks below. I repositioned myself so my feet were on the back wall and my hands on the front wall again, and continued the precarious traverse.

Maybe I could just pretend it never happened. After all, I'd never see anyone from Ipktu again. What had happened was my secret.

Except I'd always know.

The next time I would raise my arm to hurt another goblin, I'd remember the Slashers raising their claws against me, and the Bandit King's voice calling them off.

The next time I lusted to punish my enemies, I'd remember that I deserved death and the Bandit King had not given it to me.

Hatred for anyone would be hypocritical. Revenge was unthinkable.

The Bandit King had ruined everything.

I shifted all my weight to one arm, working my way around a gap in the flowstone.

If only the Slashers *had* killed me. To live my life in the aftermath of what he'd done, my whole existence a reminder of a debt I could never repay—it stripped me of every ounce of pride. It would be better to die, to—

The hand supporting my weight slipped. I swung my other arm and tried to catch the wall, but my claws missed.

I pitched forward. My head hit the stone as I plummeted onto the jagged rocks below.

My left arm took the brunt of the fall, and I heard a loud crack beneath me as I crumpled onto the slag. For a moment the pain paralyzed me, and I lay panting in the dark.

Broken. My arm was *broken*.

Panic set in. This kind of injury was bad under any circumstances, but here in this cave—it was fatal.

I could endure any pain if needed, but a broken bone was unusable. And there was no way I could climb out of this slippery ravine with just one arm.

I'd wished for death, and it found me.

My breath came in raggedy gasps, and hot tears sprung to my eyes. But I wouldn't cry, not here, not ever.

Calm down, Valshara. I closed my eyes and did my calming exercise—the one about death, ironically. Back in the Pit, I would imagine my soul escaping my hurting body, and it always gave me an odd sense of relief.

Breathing deeply, I pictured my floating spirit. There it was, as it had always been—a spindly, soot-black wraith with razor claws and twisted teeth. I liked to imagine it rising up, then whipping through the tunnels like a whirlwind, heading straight for the wardens' quarters. I knew which wardens my ghost would attack first, and had rehearsed how those claws and teeth could cause the most suffering.

But then, in my mind's eye, something else rose up beside the wraith. It was a small ball of orange light—a flame. The wraith shrank back from it.

"What are you?" I whispered. This was not part of my exercise.

The part of you that wants to live, the flame seemed to say.

"Too late. I'm dying now."

The little fire reddened. *You want to die,* it accused. *If you can't hurt people anymore, then you'll just curl up and surrender to death.*

I clenched my fist. "But they hurt *me*. Not just the wardens, the whole goblin society. They locked me up and threw me away. It's my right to punish them for the suffering they inflicted."

Revenge won't undo your pain. What will it accomplish?

I stopped. I'd thirsted to pay back these evils for years—but I'd never thought to ask why. "I don't know. I ... I don't have anything else to hope for."

You have a second chance.

I paused, remembering the Bandit King's strange words: "I steal you away from darkness. I buy you for light. You are new."

Assuming I somehow survived this injury—which was unlikely—was it really so simple to just start over?

The little fire grew brighter, and the wraith version of me shrank further back.

But if you want to live, you must do so as a pardoned criminal —not the judge, not the executioner. You cannot live by mercy and also demand revenge. Choose.

I glanced once more at the wraith, noticing for the first time how pitiful and one-dimensional she was. Why had I been holding onto my revenge fantasy so tightly?

After an agonizing moment, I reached out my hand to the tiny flame and let out a sob. "I want to live."

The fire touched my blood-red fingers and then lit up the entire cavern, burning so intensely I squeezed my eyes shut.

When I opened them a moment later, the vision was gone, and I was once again in unbroken darkness.

"I do," I sobbed. "I want to live."

At last I let the tears flow—the tears held back from six years' worth of pain. They rushed down my face, hot on my cheeks. They soaked into the stones below and were gone.

I lifted my left hand to wipe them away. Pain shot through my arm.

My heart beat faster. My left arm. I could move it. I could wiggle my fingers.

It wasn't broken. Putting pressure on it felt like I was stabbing it with a knife, but I could still do it.

I was going to *live*.

The trouble wasn't over yet, of course. I activated my red light to examine the two walls of wet flowstone above. Traversing them horizontally was difficult, but trying to climb up to reach the entrance of the tunnel eight feet above was going to be a much bigger issue.

Laying my head back on the bed of fallen rocks, I heard it—just for a second.

I tilted my head again, trying to pinpoint the sound. Running water, coming from somewhere below me, the soft gurgle detectable only at one particular angle.

I shone my fingers at the jagged floor. There—a small crack in the bottom of the V. The limestone was so thin it was almost translucent, worn away by centuries of dripping water. The faint blue glow of moss illuminated the space below.

Grabbing a loose rock, I lifted it high and bashed it into the paper-thin limestone.

The rock surface crackled. I hit it again and slivers of stone tumbled into the black tunnel beneath me. I heard the pebbles splash gently into unseen water.

I will live.

I smashed the rock over and over until my knuckles bled, until I had an opening wide enough.

Twisting my aching body, I worked my feet through the hole. The edges of the broken limestone scraped my skin like blades, but I didn't care. I hooked my arms over the razor-sharp edges, worked my shoulders through, turned my head, and let myself drop.

Splash.

The cool water soothed my scraped skin. I sat in the middle of a shallow stream, faintly illuminated by phosphorescent moss. I knelt and let the water flow over my battered knees and legs, grinning like a child.

I'm alive.

More alive than I'd been in six long years—maybe more alive than I'd ever been. I dipped the Bandit King's mug into the water and took a long, quenching drink. Looking up into the narrow crack I'd just struggled through, I decided that as far as I was concerned, the broken body of Valshara the convict remained up there, dead, taking her hatred and list of revenges to the grave with her.

Now I was someone new, as innocent as a justborn. I secured the mug to my belt and rose to my feet.

And the first miracle of my new life was that I stood at that precise moment.

Something whizzed by my knee, in the spot where my shoulder had just been. It clattered against a stalagmite a foot away from me. I squinted at it in the faint blue light and my blood turned to ice.

A dart.

A poison dart.

The signature weapon of the Faceless.

5

FLIGHT IN THE DARK

I dashed down the stream bed in a blind panic, dodging stalactites hanging from the low ceiling. I splashed noisily, cursing as my feet slipped on underwater stones.

This was no time for stealth—just a desperate bid to put distance between me and him, hoping his darts had a limited range.

The Faceless—the rising shadow, the unrelenting hunter, the inescapable pursuer of Blood Hands.

The Faceless had found me.

Of course he had. I was bashing that rock so loudly it must have echoed through the whole Dominion. He must have tracked the sound and waited for me to drop right in front of his tranquilizing blow-dart.

My heart pounded in my throat as I stumbled through the water. The stream grew deeper, fed by tiny waterfalls flowing out of the rock walls around me.

The water sloshed around my knees, and I leapt belly-first into the stream, doing my best to swim as rocks scraped my underside. Swimming was good—not only did the current help propel me along, but the lower profile made me a more difficult target.

Moss-light was sparse here, and I almost didn't see the cave ceiling plunge down into the stream ahead. I drew a quick breath and dove beneath the water, one hand feeling the rock face above. I prayed the ceiling would rise back above water level before I drowned.

Mercifully, it did. I resurfaced to find myself in an enormous cavern room filled with glowing moss. Thousands of spindly stalactites hung from a ceiling fifty feet above me. Some had grown long enough to reach the uneven cave floor, forming thick pillars of rope-like stone.

Around me, the water swirled in a pool with no obvious exit point.

My body tensed. *Trapped in the open.*

The Faceless was going to rise up from the pool any second and find me sputtering here. I leapt out of the water, fretting over the tell-tale puddles I left on the pale limestone floor. I darted behind one of the largest pillars.

Not enough—still too easy to find. I dug my claws into the limestone pillar and hoisted myself upward, scaling the slippery stone as fast as I dared.

It was only when I had climbed about halfway that I reflected on my strategy.

I didn't have one. Typical.

Well, I was committed now. I reached for the next twist of rock, trying not to think about what would happen to my bones if I fell from this height.

Adding to my distress was my left arm—not broken, but still protesting with pain. Too much strain and it could give out on me, sending me to the stone floor below.

I swallowed and continued climbing, letting my right arm do all the pulling and using my left arm to stabilize only. The stone was slick but offered plenty of nooks and crannies where stalactites had fused together over the years.

At last I reached the cavern ceiling.

Great.

Stupid.

Now what? I scanned the ceiling above and noticed a darker-than-expected crack. Wait—could it be a natural chimney?

I inched around the pillar. Yes, that crack was a vertical shaft, though from where I clung to the pillar I couldn't tell how far up it extended.

Reaching my hand out, I felt the air stir. A draft meant there was an opening at the top.

I strained my body upward and the claws of my good arm dug into a recess in the side of the chimney wall. In one heart-wrenching movement, I let go of the pillar, my body dangling in the open air.

Uggh. I found a hold with my left hand and used the strength of my right arm to hoist myself into the chimney. My feet scrambled against the wall and found footholds.

I'd made it. Now all I had to do was keep climbing and not fall to my death. Good thing my left arm was throbbing in pain.

Inch by inch I ascended, trying to feel out holds in the dark tunnel. My clawed toes dug into the stone surfaces on either side, and I relied on my legs to do most of the lifting so that my arm wouldn't betray me.

Something made a *clink* down below. I held my breath.

The Faceless was in the cavern.

The thin opening of the chimney was my only window into the glowing cavern below me. If I couldn't see him, I reasoned, then he couldn't see me. Surely from the floor of that enormous room he wouldn't notice the crack in the—

A shadow blotted out the blue light below, just for a second. Someone had definitely moved down there.

My heart skipped about three beats before I could take a breath.

Focus on the task at hand.

My eyes strained in the darkness. Up above, I could see a faint outline, a change in the light. Only ten more feet or so and I'd get out of this chimney, away from the Faceless.

I held my breath and repositioned, my hand feeling out my next hold. I'd do this as quickly as possible. I glanced down one more time to make sure I had a steady place to for my feet. Just as I was ready—

A hand.

A black hand appeared at the bottom of the chimney, grabbing a stone. A shadowy body followed—the features indistinct but definitely goblin.

He'd found me.

I pushed my feet off of the wall so fast I practically threw myself up onto the next grip. My fingers slipped for a moment, but I pinched hard and caught myself. I scrambled for the next one.

Below, the Faceless has already climbed five feet, his movements smooth and swift.

I scrambled up to the next hold, reckless now. A rock wobbled beneath my grasp. I lunged for another one, just as the loose rock sheared off the wall and clattered down the chimney. With any luck, it would hit my purser on the way down.

My left arm strained for the next reach. Pain shot from my elbow to my shoulder as I pulled my body weight up.

One more yard. I could almost reach the opening above.

The Faceless' breath stirred against the soles of my feet.

With a burst of energy, I propelled myself through the opening above. The rock pinched around my hips.

Claws brushed my foot just as I grabbed onto a nearby stalagmite and yanked myself out of the hole, the edges digging into my thighs so hard I was sure it took an inch off either side.

One quick flash of my red light revealed a stone floor littered with rocks. I grabbed the biggest one, smashed it over the opening, and heard the Faceless curse.

The narrow room before me forked into two tunnels. My instinct was to go for the one on the right—it was smaller and less open. Instead I extinguished my light and sprinted to the one on the left, hoping that by defying instinct I'd throw the Faceless off.

The tunnel was pitch-black but I forged ahead, navigating by feel alone—one hand running along the rough tunnel wall, my feet shuffling and feeling for loose rocks and stalagmites. I held my uninjured arm in front of my face to prevent serious injury from rock overhangs and stalactites.

Under any other circumstances, it would be stupid to move this fast in the dark, but I had no choice. I bashed my toes and bruised my arms but still I pushed on.

It was the smell that hit me first—a wave of ammonia that brought tears to my eyes. I suppressed a gag. What could be—?

Then I heard it—a chittering sound, coming from above.

Bats.

I'd stumbled into a bat colony, and the stench and sound were overwhelming. It was disgustingly ... perfect.

Perfect.

The smell of droppings and the bats' chatter would mask my passage. I picked up my pace, far less afraid of making noise.

The bats grew louder above me as they woke up. It was feeding time.

Hope leapt within me. Bats fly to the aboveground world to feast on insects. A bat colony meant I was near the end of the cavern system. They were about to show me my escape route.

If I could get Topside, I might be able to throw the Faceless off for good. The cave system offered only a handful of possible paths at any given time, at best. But the aboveground world was wide open. As unpleasant and extreme as the environment would be, it would provide an unlimited number of escape routes.

I. Love. Bats.

As if sensing my gratitude, a few dozen bats swooped down from the teeming ceiling and fluttered past me. I ran behind them, following them down a hidden side tunnel. More bats swooped past me as though to say, "This way, follow us."

Up ahead I saw a tinge of light—not blue moss, but pale light from the Topside world. My escape from this nightmare was close.

The screeches and chittering grew louder around me, and I felt leathery wings brush against my arms. I could now make out the outlines of the bats' furry little bodies and their smush-nosed faces.

I continued my exhilarating sprint, the light growing brighter at the end of the tunnel ahead. All at once we burst out into an illuminated cavern room. The bats beat their wings, lifting up away around me.

My feet slowed. *No.*

The bats rose up toward a hole in the cavern ceiling and disappeared into the dusk.

I fell to my knees.

The large cavern had only one exit, and it was far above me. There were no walls close enough to scale, no pillars to climb. The only way out was by flight. The bats brushed past, ignoring my outstretched hands.

I couldn't retrace my path now—there was only a matter of time before—

The needled point of the dart sank into my shoulder. Within seconds, I felt the tranquilizer working its way through my blood, tingling as it went. Even then I tried to run, but I made it only a few steps before I collapsed onto the stone floor.

The last thing I saw was the opening in the ceiling, where a star twinkled in the indigo sky, so far away.

6

THE FACELESS

My head hurt, and it hurt multiple ways. First there was a dull ache near the base of my skull, like something was swollen. That was probably an after-effect of the tranquilizer.

My temples also throbbed—again, tranquilizer—and something lay taut against my neck.

Not just my neck—my entire body was restrained.

I eased open an eye. A lattice of grey rope bound me to a thin board against my back. A cave ceiling clipped by, stalactites pointing directly toward me.

Closing my eyes again, I fought a wave of nausea. How could I be moving while lying down? The last thing I remembered was a cave full of bats, and something piercing my shoulder.

My pulse quickened. While I had been unconscious, someone had tied me down to a cave sled and was now dragging it across the cavern floor. And that person was ...

In a panic, I strained my arms and legs, but the ropes held me firm. My movements were jerky and unpredictable—the tranquilizer's effect hadn't completely worn off.

"Prisoner One-Eight-Six-Two," said a silky voice in the darkness.

The sled slowed to a stop, and a dark shape loomed over me.

The Faceless.

Even backlit against the moss light he was difficult to see. The black cloth that covered every inch of his skin had a fuzzy texture that blurred his silhouette.

When he crossed his arms against his body, the cloth absorbed so much light that I could no longer see where his arms ended and the rest of his body began.

"Don't resist." Dark fabric obscured his face entirely, and the voice floated from unseen lips. "I'll just dose you again. Besides, even if you could get through six feet of spider-cord, you're in no condition to fight. It's been what, four days since you've eaten?"

Actually, it hadn't been that long, thanks to the plate of root mash in Ipktu.

He doesn't know about Ipktu, I realized. The flight through the caves had left my new clothes mud-stained and frayed. *Oh, he doesn't know about Ipktu, and as long as I keep my mouth closed, the Bandit King and his people are safe.*

The Faceless reached into a fold in his black tunic, pulling out a wicked-looking dart.

I squirmed in the ropes, anticipating the needle. I had to delay him. "Why do you hide your face?"

The black form straightened a little. "I have nothing to hide. But as a Blood Hand, you have lost the privilege of gazing upon a Guidelight's face."

Ah. Of course the Faceless would be a Guidelight. Who else would hunt us so ruthlessly?

The Guidelights had presented themselves as champions of the people, leading an uprising that defeated the Masters. But they turned traitor, emerging from negotiations with a new story: the Guidelight rebellion had always been against the Blood Hand police force, not the Masters that employed us. The Guidelights joined forces with the Masters, claiming the role of moral counselors for their oppressive rule. Meanwhile we Blood Hands were tried en masse and cast into the Pit.

"Wait," I said. "You were at the trials."

The blank mask gave no sign of acknowledgement, but I continued anyway.

"Don't you remember me? At the trials? Valshara Valshayan." My father's name burned my tongue as I spoke it. "The only female Blood Hand on the force. The captains refused to let me participate in most of the raids and arrests, so the judge gave me only five years. I've been counting days. I've served at least five and a half." I swallowed. "So, legally, you have to let me go."

The black silhouette made no movement. "In all your time in the Pit, have you ever seen a prisoner freed?"

My heart sank. Of course I hadn't. Once the wardens got you in their power, not even your corpse left the Pit. Our trials had been for public show, the sentences meaningless. Had I really been so naïve?

"A properly run society," the Faceless continued, "must praise the righteous, and condemn the wicked to torment. Permanently."

Panic welled up within me. "Please—I've suffered so much already. Tell them One-Eight-Six-Two broke her arm and died in the caverns. I'll leave the Dominion and never come back. I'll never hurt another goblin as long as I live, I swear it."

"No power on earth could change a Blood Hand into anything but a criminal," he said. "You will return to the Pit."

I writhed against my restraints. "Can you show no mercy?"

"Mercy," the Faceless scoffed. "Mercy is immoral. It's incompatible with my oath as a Guidelight—to perform works of righteousness, no matter the personal cost."

He pulled back his sleeve, revealing a green arm covered with burn scars. Each scar stretched exactly one inch, arranged into a pattern that coiled down his forearm. The older scars on his biceps were a faded purple, while the ones further down were bright red, the last few still raw and inflamed.

I grimaced.

"I have never failed in my duty." He pointed to an old scar. "I earned this one for Prisoner Nine-Four-Seven, returned to the Pit after only three hours on the run." He traced his finger down the spiral. "This was Eight-Nine-Four, who somehow got hold of a knife and nearly removed my hand. He died in the Pit a month after our encounter, I believe.

"This was for One-Six-Zero-Seven, and this is Six-Five-One. And this space here ..." He pointed to a patch of unmarked skin on his inner forearm, beside his most recent burn. "Tomorrow at this time I'll have a scar for you, Prisoner One-Eight-Six-Two."

He rolled his sleeve down and took up his dart again, dipping its tip into a small vial. "I am compelled to suffer for my duty, just as you are compelled to suffer for your crimes."

Instead of simply injecting me with the needle, the Faceless loaded the dart into his blowgun and drew it to his hidden lips.

Seriously? Beneath my restraints, every muscle in my body tensed, bracing for high-speed impact.

"Now," he said, his voice almost a purr. "No more talk. Sleep."

The dart hit with an audible *thwack*. But here was the second miracle of my new life: the needle lodged itself in my rough-woven belt. The poison tip reached my skin at an angle and just barely pierced me.

The numbing agent moved through my body, but only as a pins-and-needles sensation that quickly subsided.

Maybe it was because of the lattice of rope restraints, but the Faceless didn't notice that the dart protruded from my belt, not my flesh. I rolled my eyes back and feigned going limp, and he looked no closer.

The floor moved below me as he took up the rope by my feet and resumed dragging the sled.

So. I had an advantage. The Faceless assumed I would be unconscious for some time—maybe a few hours. The down side was that I couldn't make any movement without giving my secret away.

I waited.

The rope that bound me was indeed spider coil—a weave of

spider silk and copper filaments that was stronger than iron and nearly impossible to cut. Even if I could get my obsidian shiv from my hidden pocket, it would do no good.

Keeping my eyes closed, I tried to make sense of the pattern of ropes against my body. Where was the knot?

The Faceless dragged me along for a painful hour. The thin board beneath me glided over rough surfaces, but couldn't shield me from the rocks he made no effort to avoid.

I detected a change in the soundscape. An underground stream splashed over stones, the ceiling of the tunnel echoing back in chirps.

Frigid water seeped up through the board. Cold water rose above my arms and legs and splashed above my ears, but went no higher.

The Faceless wouldn't let me drown—a dead Blood Hand probably wouldn't earn him a pain badge—but apparently he didn't care if I got a little hypothermia. Maybe that's why one of his previous victims died within a month of his return.

Without realizing it, I'd tensed my muscles and clenched my fists. I tried to relax and look unconscious again, but then I realized—with the stream water flowing over me, he wouldn't notice a little movement.

My fingers set to work, cautiously searching for the knot that held the ropes taut. There—just above my navel.

I recognized it as a skull-knot from my military training. I dug my claw into the bottommost loop and wiggled it. The ropes crisscrossing my body slackened. I tugged a few more times, loosening the ropes just enough that I could slip out when the right opportunity came.

What exactly that opportunity would look like I didn't know. I wouldn't be able to get far without the Faceless hitting me with a dart.

I'd have to plan this carefully. Nothing impulsive this time.

The river current grew stronger, battering my cave sled and nearly tearing the guide rope out of my captor's grasp. But no such luck. A few moments later I was hoisted onto a stone bank, and the Faceless resumed dragging my soaked carcass along the ground.

But the tunnel floor was much more even here. It was brighter, too, and the light had a green tinge to it.

We were within the boundaries of the Dominion again. Green phosphorescent mushrooms were cultivated at regular intervals along major throughways, giving more light than the wild mosses.

I detected the scent of goblins in the tunnels ahead. Over the roar of the river beside me, I could hear indistinct voices.

With every step we took, my chances for escape dwindled.

7

THE RED CLOAK

T he goblin chatter grew louder and the familiar scents more intense. The Faceless stopped, and I heard several subdued conversations nearby. A minute passed, and the Faceless dragged my sled forward a foot or two. Then we stopped again.

Were we waiting in line? Ah—we must have reached a checkpoint.

The Masters had checkpoints throughout the Dominion, adding more as their paranoia grew. They wanted eyes everywhere.

The river rushed on beside our line of goblins, and I could hear it crashing down over the edge of a cliff. I opened my eyes a crack and could see mist rising from the waterfall, glowing green in the mushroom light.

The Masters loved a dramatic backdrop.

In the corner of my eye, I noticed a few goblin shapes lean over to look at me. But an immobilized prisoner wasn't that unusual of a sight in the Dominion, and they lost interest.

A shadow fell across my stretcher. An enormous lizard shuffled by on stubby crocodile legs, tickling me with its blue tongue.

Somehow I managed not to flinch. Giant skinks have particularly nasty bites, with teeth that inject a painful venom while they tear flesh.

The beast's handler yanked on its chain and pulled it away from me, leading it further down the growing line of goblins.

Security must have tightened if they had skink patrols at a standard checkpoint. Of course, I'd missed six years of changes while I was in the Pit.

We moved forward another two feet and stopped.

At the front of the line would be a member of the Masters party, wearing a long cloak in a rusty red color. The Masters claimed they soaked the fabric in the blood of rebels, but I recalled my mother coloring my father's cloak with a mix of ammonia and devil's toe mushroom.

With the heavy presence of Masters and the skink patrols breathing down our necks, this was the worst place to attempt escape. I'd continue feigning unconsciousness until we passed the checkpoint.

Of course, if I made a run for it later, I'd have to work my way back through here.

As I fretted over my shrinking list of options, I heard someone chortle—an arrogant laugh I'd recognize anywhere.

Old Master Sayek. Could it be that after all these years, he was still in power? Doubtless he still enjoyed every chance to debase the weaker goblins around him.

When I was a child, my father had entertained him a few times in our home. Old Sayek loved to boast about cruel things he'd done to Lowblood families. The lurid accounts of his abuse had kept me sleepless for weeks. Old Sayek might have been telling one of those stories now, based the raucous laughter.

"Isn't that right, Snivel?" he asked.

"If you say so, my lord."

Lady Sayek—was she here, too? Masters' wives didn't often appear in public.

Old Sayek was always coming up with cruel nicknames for his

wife, who was about fifteen years his junior. She always answered demurely, with a practiced smile and a vacant look in her eyes.

Even as a child that empty look had haunted me. It was Lady Sayek's eyes that had driven me into a career in the police— anything to escape her fate of a political marriage.

"Next."

The line moved again. I kept my eyes half-closed, focusing on a limping goblin in front of me. He leaned on a crutch, his hand fidgeting nervously at his side.

Meanwhile, the river rushed past us toward the waterfall, roaring as it plunged over the edge.

"Next."

The limping goblin now approached Old Master Sayek. He straightened and lifted his crutch.

I couldn't turn my head to see, but I heard a blade being drawn.

"Hey," came Old Sayek's voice, "What's the—?"

Shouts from the patrol guards, screams from the crowd, and the hungry grunts of skinks filled the cavern. Goblins of all ranks rushed toward the attack—some to help, others most likely to watch a Master get taken down.

Even my Faceless captor pushed forward into the fray, leaving me unattended.

Now.

I sprang out of the cave sled, the loosened restraints falling away easily. Keeping close to the floor, I scrambled through the feet of the crowd and toward freedom.

An ear-splitting scream rang out. Lady Sayek.

I turned to see her falling, knocked backward by the crush of the crowd trying to grab her husband's attacker.

Her rust-red cloak fluttered mid-air for a second before she hit the river. The current swept her toward the cliff.

Just before the whitewater pulled her under, I caught a glimpse of the terror in her eyes.

Those haunted eyes that had stayed with me since girlhood.

I pivoted mid-stride and wove back through the crowd toward the stony river edge.

Too late. Her arms rose from the waves, grasping at nothing, and she dropped over the edge of the waterfall.

Her scream echoed through the chamber, rising through the green mist—and then choked off.

I reached the cliff's edge and looked over. Water plunged thirty feet, crashing into a black river below.

There—just beside the thundering cascade, about halfway down, the rust-red cloak hung from a protruding rock. Beneath it dangled Lady Sayek, clutching at the fabric growing tighter around her neck.

The red cloak had saved her from the fall, but now it strangled her.

I dropped my legs over the rock face, the water crashing beside me. I began my descent recklessly and almost paid for it. My hands slipped on the water-smoothed stones and I nearly tumbled backward into the chasm.

The waterfall roared just a foot from my side, threatening to sweep me to my death if I got too close.

This down-climb was harder than the chimney I'd scaled before my capture. It definitely didn't help that among the onlookers who'd gathered at the top of the precipice, I could see the indistinct outline of the Faceless.

He drew a dart from his black clothing.

"No." A soldier pulled his gloved hand back. "See? She's saving Sayek's wife."

The gagging sounds grew louder from below, and I wondered how much time I had before Lady Sayek lost consciousness. As I struggled to find my next hold, I could feel the strength draining from my injured arm.

Not good.

By the time I reached the rock overhang, her eyes had started to roll back in her head. I grabbed Lady Sayek's flailing arm, trying to hoist her up. She took a rasping breath as the pressure around her throat relieved.

I pulled her onto the overhang, tears stinging as my arm protested in pain. The crowd above cheered.

Lady Sayek coughed and gagged for a full minute, tearing at the iron brooch that fastened her cloak. I helped her work the long iron pin loose from the red linen. Once it was free, she flung the cloak into the chasm. It floated in the green mist, hovering like a red ghost for a moment, then fluttered down into the black river.

I saw its brooch gleam on the water's surface. Then the cloak darted toward the cliff wall and winked away.

I blinked. Why had the cloak moved toward the rocks, against the river current?

Lady Sayek continued to wheeze, and I waited for her to pull herself together. We still had a treacherous ascent to make.

The crowd perched on the edge of the cliff above continued to shout encouragement. Whatever had happened to Master Sayek and his attacker, their attention was now on us.

I felt a small glimmer of hope. Maybe this is how I would escape the Pit—a hero's pardon.

When Lady Sayek could breathe normally again, I put my hand on her shoulder. "Are you ready to go?"

She nodded, grasping my hand. Then her fingers stiffened.

"Oh—you're a Blood Hand." Her voice held an edge of disgust.

And I knew at that moment that in the eyes of Dominion society, there was no path of redemption for me. Even if I brought Lady Sayek safely to the top of the cliff, one glimpse at my red-stained fingers would likely turn the crowd against me—fast and violently. It had already happened in Ipktu.

And then the Faceless would tranquilize me and I'd wake up again in the Pit.

I swallowed back a growing lump in my throat. What had

gotten into me? My one chance to escape the Pit, and I'd thrown it away for this.

Maybe I could use Lady Sayek as a bargaining chip, demanding that they release me or I'd chuck her over the cliff myself.

But something inside me recoiled at the thought. Hadn't I sworn off harming another goblin? Besides, even if I carried through with that plan, the Faceless could still just shoot me.

Black water churned below us. If I dropped into the river now, I might survive. But it would be simple for the Faceless to track where I—or my body—ended up, so there was no point in the risk.

Nowhere to go but up.

Lady Sayek watched me, her eyes still with that haunted look.

I sighed. "Look, I can't carry you. You're going to have to climb." I pointed at her long skirt and finely knitted slippers. "Those aren't going to help."

She dutifully peeled off the wet slippers and tucked up her skirt.

I guided her bare foot into a crack in the rock face, then got underneath her to boost her toward a protruding stone she could grab.

We had only been climbing for a minute when her inexperienced fingers slipped. She fell, landing on my chest. Somehow I managed to hold onto the cliffside, cradling her with my body and wincing in pain.

If we didn't figure this out, she was going to kill us both.

"Grab that square rock," I said through my teeth. "Dig your claws in before shifting your weight."

Lady Sayek obeyed. She trembled as she lifted herself upward, step by painstaking step.

Slowly we made our way upward—toward safety for her and an inescapable fate for me.

And all I could think about was that stupid red cloak. Where did it go? What had drawn it toward the cliff face?

We were now just a foot or two from the crowded ledge. I could see the Faceless waiting, his gloved hands fingering his weapon.

I had to push Lady Sayek the last little bit of the way. Dozens of goblin arms reach out to grab her hands.

And as they lifted her off my shoulders, I guessed what had happened to the cloak. If I was right, it was a piece of information that could save my life.

As soon as Lady Sayek was safely on solid ground above me, the Faceless moved forward, his blowgun at his invisible lips.

Now or never.

I raised my hand as though to grab onto the cliff ledge, but let the rock slip out from beneath my fingers. I lurched backward, making a show of trying to regain my balance.

And right before the horrified crowd, I plummeted to my death.

8

IRON PIN

Only it wasn't really to my death.

I hoped.

At the last frantic moment of free fall, I took a deep breath, praying it wasn't my last. I straightened my body and pierced the water like a knife, plunging into icy blackness.

The third miracle of my new life was that the rocks submerged beneath the waterfall were at a generous depth. Otherwise I would have been smashed on them—a possibility I was only now realizing.

My bare soles brushed the rough floor of stones in the cold darkness. I pushed off, fighting the force of churning water above me, swimming blindly toward the vertical cliff wall.

My numbed fingers couldn't find it.

Air was running out. Time was running out. I fought every instinct and kept myself underwater. If I resurfaced, I was lost.

Then—I felt it. A slight pull in the water, running contrary to the powerful river current.

I let the mysterious undertow pull me in, stars dancing in the corner of my vision. Exhaustion made my swimming erratic, and I bumped into stone surfaces to my left and right.

An underwater tunnel in the side of the cliff—just as I had guessed. I hoped it wasn't a dead end.

I raised my hand above me in the black water and struck an unyielding stone ceiling. I tried again, and again. On the sixth attempt, my hand shot upward, free, and my fingers felt dry air.

Not a second too soon. I kicked upward and gasped as the water fell away from my face. Treading water, I gulped air into my lungs.

When my breathing calmed, I struck the surface of the water and listened in the darkness. The echoes of the splash chirped back, quick and sharp.

A small cave, perhaps no more than an air pocket, hidden in the cliffside some thirty feet below the Masters' checkpoint.

No one knew it was here. No one knew *I* was here.

Fabric brushed against my foot in the darkness and I stifled a scream. I punched the black water and my knuckles brushed a limp linen garment.

Lady Sayek's cloak, just where I had predicted it would be. I sighed in relief and pulled it toward myself.

Something cold and hard was attached to it—the iron pin that fastened the cloak. I ran my fingers along the metal ring and felt the intricate carvings denoting the status of the Master rank.

Hold on—a Master's pin. Did I actually have a Master's pin in my possession?

This was the third miracle of my new life—or was I already on miracle number four?

A Master's pin on a red cloak would grant me safe passage anywhere in the Dominion. As long as I didn't speak, kept my face covered, and looked as though I were on serious business, no goblin would dare question me. I could walk right through the heart of the Dominion.

But first things first. I had to make sure there was a way out of this pocket-cave.

And I had to move soon. Without knowing the size of the

cave, I didn't know how much oxygen was left. How terrible to escape drowning only to suffocate in the air.

Reaching upward in the darkness, I felt for the ceiling. The surface that my fingers found was as sharp as knives.

I recoiled, treading water for a moment as I debated. There was no possible way anyone could see light from the cave's underwater entrance. And I had to know what I was dealing with.

Reluctantly, I stretched out one finger and willed my red light to glow.

A thousand red dots shone back, reflecting at every angle. I extinguished my light and the cave went black again.

I reached out again, shining my red fingers at full power. I gasped at the spectacle above me.

The entire ceiling glittered with quartz crystals. It was hard to tell the color in only dim red light, but it wasn't white, wasn't black ... was it purple?

Yes—this was an enormous amethyst cache, hidden beneath the Masters' feet. The violet crystals were valued by goblins and Topsiders alike. This cavern held more wealth than perhaps all the Masters owned together.

And then I felt something that made my heart leap for joy—a faint draft of air. I turned toward the source, holding my red hand out. Yes—on the far wall of the cavern I spotted the mouth of a tunnel. Moving air was a sure sign it was connected to other passageways.

I was going to live.

I reached up to the ceiling and pinched a crystal, wiggling it loose. I stuffed it into my linen pocket, then grabbed for another.

As I filled my small pockets with as many gems as they could hold, I formulated my plan.

No doubt the Faceless would scour the river up and down the Dominion, searching for my body. Let him search—he'd never find this place.

He wouldn't readily give up, but eventually his superiors would re-assign him to another escapee.

I would wait him out.

I'd follow this tunnel to wherever it took me. If it led to unin-habited caves, I'd find a way to survive on lichen and millipedes. If it brought me to some distant corner of the Dominion or even to the Topside world, so be it. I'd exile myself for a few months, maybe even a year, using the gems to fund my living and to quiet the questions of any nosy people.

Then I'd skirt the edges of the Dominion, using the Master's pin to travel undisturbed.

And ultimately, I'd find a way back to Ipktu.

I looped the cloak around my neck, securing it with the iron pin, and swam toward the tunnel. The faint draft brushed across my face.

"All right," I whispered. "Take me wherever you lead."

This cave tunnel carved by running water was far wider and more comfortable than the tiny cracks I'd squeezed through earlier. The rocky floor rose as soon as I left the pocket-cave, and I found myself able to wade against the stream's current.

Anytime I came to a fork with multiple passages, I chose the ones that were largest, angled upward, or had the more powerful stream flowing through them.

I managed to catch a few cave shrimp and eyeless fish on the way, and while they tasted terrible, they kept me going. When I found dry places—a narrow sandy bank, a large stone in the middle of the stream—I'd sleep in snatches.

Who knows how many days I travelled? I had no way to mark the passage of time. The stream dwindled to a trickle, and I found myself climbing up broken boulders and through wide tunnels of sleeping bats.

And as I crawled through one passageway, I could see my hands, my arms, the red in my cloak. This wasn't a blue pinpoint of moss, but a grey light that illuminated the entire cave.

My heart pounded with both joy and fear.

There, up ahead, stood a beaming circle of light that marked the end of the cavern system. I squinted against its power and crawled toward it. A warm breeze tickled the tips of my ears.

I hesitated for a moment, then made my way out to the Topside world.

9

THE CHANGELING CHILD

P ushing away fat vines, I squeezed out of a hole in the side of a rocky hill.

For a moment all I could see was green—a green so vivid it made the Dominion's pale mushroom light seem pathetic.

Other colors gradually came into view, so intense they seemed unreal. I didn't even have names for some of them.

The one time I'd been Topside before, I'd come out on a bare mountaintop. But this place teemed with life, with more varieties of stems and fronds and leaves than I'd even known existed.

Beside me, shaggy vines twisted around some sort of pillar—a greyish brown cylinder of textured stone. As I squinted at the landscape around me, I realized these grey pillars were one of the primary features of this place.

The ground beneath me was curiously soft. Moisture from crushed mosses soaked the bottom of my clawed feet, while some sort of frilly plant tickled my legs and back. Unpleasant, to say the least.

Oh, and the *smells*. Plant resin. The rot of decay. The musk of unseen creatures. I almost turned and went back into the tunnel right then.

Then the sun rose, its intense light searing my eyes and washing everything out in a burning orange.

Welcome to my new home. Step one: don't go blind.

My hands felt my way toward one of the strange grey pillars—the surface was a little too soft to be stone—and I ducked behind it, cowering in its shade. But the light Topside was so persistent that even shadows didn't offer much protection.

I stumbled toward a cluster of shrubs, pushing my way beneath the thin branches and crouching in the shade of their many leaves.

The thicket made a decent shelter, at least temporarily. I curled myself up in a bed of dead leaves and pungent soil and pondered my next challenge.

Step two: don't starve.

What exactly was I going to eat up here?

Something prickled against my arm and I was disgusted to find a thin plant with spikes—literal spikes—along its stem.

Seriously?

I grabbed a thornless section of the plant's stem—not on my first try, alas—and yanked the briar up. In the hole left in the earth, several beetles scurried away.

Hold on. Scratching the soil with my claw, I uncovered more beetles and a worm. Gross, but edible.

Bug life was more plentiful here than I had anticipated. That, at least, was good news.

My exhaustion caught up with me. Pulling the red hood of my Master's cloak over my face, I dozed beneath the thicket shelter. When I awoke, the light was far less intense, and I emerged from beneath the bush and stood in the dusk.

How could anyone bear a world where the light changes so dramatically? Did it do this every day?

But now that the light had gotten bearable, the noise ratcheted up. I covered my ears against a cacophony of chirps and rattles and croaks, emanating from the throats of a thousand unseen creatures.

Hopefully some of them were good to eat.

I slunk around the strange landscape, driven by hunger more than by curiosity. One surprising discovery: the immense grey pillars weren't stone, but stems of a gigantic plant, covered with a rough but yielding material. If I pulled off the outer layer, I often found caches of insects hiding inside.

The stiff plant material gave off a resinous aroma that was almost pleasant to my overwhelmed nose.

I moved onto another giant plant—one with an especially wide stem—and pried off some of its outer cover. An acrid odor stung my nostrils, so strong that I clapped my hands over my face.

The smell burned through my sinuses, tingling and stinging. It reminded me of the caustic fumes that came out of the Pit ore furnaces.

I stumbled away from the pillar-like plant, but one of its branches whipped down and grabbed me by the cloak.

The branch hoisted me mid-air. I wedged my hand between the cloak collar and my throat to prevent it from strangling me. The rough surface of the pillar shimmered for a moment, and a woman stepped out.

She was human-like, but only three feet tall—only a little shorter than me. Leaves formed her hair, and her glowing green eyes scowled.

"How dare you attack my tree?" she scolded in Vindorian.

"*Tree?*" I repeated the unfamiliar word. "I not know *tree.*"

The woman pointed to the grey pillar behind her. "This tree, you stupid thing." She furrowed her brow. "What kind of creature are you?"

"I goblin." I struggled to recall basic Vindorian words. "I not know *tree.* I not know many stuffs about Topside."

The branch holding my cloak lowered me to the ground, and I found myself crouching at the strange woman's feet. The leaves in her hair rustled, and she regarded me with curiosity.

"Do you know what I am?"

I gave her my best guess. "You not a man."

She threw back her leafy head and laughed. "Oh, lost little goblin, you are very *nuh-ruh-ruh.*"

She didn't actually say *nuh-ruh-ruh*, but she was speaking so quickly I couldn't keep up. Vindorian has all of these strange "uh" sounds in it, and speakers often blend the words together.

The little woman continued. "I'll give you some advice. I am a Wood Elf, and if you attack a Wood Elf's tree, we attack you with magic."

"*Magic*? I not know *magic.*"

The elf waved her hands and the tree branches whipped down toward me. The burning sensation returned to my sinuses.

"Oh," I said, slapping my hand over my nose. "I know *magic*. I stay away."

"Good. Because there are many more of my kind here in Woodshea."

"I not know *Wood Shed.*"

The elf spread her arms wide. "Woodshea, this forest. This—" She must have seen my next question forming. "—place of many trees. It's a dangerous place for mortals like yourself."

"I not know—"

"Mortals—people without magic, like you. People who can die. Leave Woodshea. Go back home, goblin."

Yeah, not likely. "Yes, yes. I go," I said, waving dismissively. "Thanks you for advices."

I slunk away, keeping close to the ground. Without knowing what other kinds of creatures lived in this crazy world, it seemed wise to keep a low profile. I gave the trunks wide berth as I shuffled over the forest floor. Something tiny leapt onto the path—some sort of pudgy salamander with giant legs for jumping.

This looked promising as a food source, though the creature proved difficult to catch. I chased it some distance, winding around the trunk of a large tree.

Around the other side fluttered the red cloak of a Master. I stifled a scream.

Wait—it was just a scrap of red cloth caught in a bush.

I exhaled and approached it. The cloth was tattered and threadbare, and several of the bush's branches had grown right through its moth-holes.

The dye had faded, but it appeared to have originally been a deep and brilliant red—not the rusty color of devil's toe dye. A parade of circles and triangles danced along it, embroidered in tiny golden threads.

The cloth smelled like leaves and soil and forest air, with no trace of its original wearer.

I moved on, trying to figure out where that jumpy salamander had gone. A grassy clearing opened up in the middle of the trees, revealing a welcome sight—a circle of fat white mushrooms.

I didn't know much about Topside fungus, but my nose could pick out toxins fairly easily. My mouth watered as I approached.

I gave the first one I came to a sniff, but it was so small I couldn't pick up much. I leaned over it to get closer to the next one.

And oh, the burn was unbearable. Sixty times as potent as the magic smell from the Wood Elf's tree.

Tears sprang to my eyes, and I stumbled back. The pain stopped.

But the magic smell hadn't come from the mushrooms—it had been in the air itself. And here I was, a foot away, and I couldn't detect a trace of the aroma.

My curiosity—or stupidity, I'm not sure which—got the better of me. I stepped over the mushrooms and into the grassy clearing they encircled.

The caustic odor almost knocked me off my feet. But that wasn't the only thing that changed inside the mushroom ring. Where seconds earlier the night had been dark, now the air glowed in a sparkling gold.

Pinching my nostrils, I squinted in the brilliant light. In a moment I could make out the shapes of people.

Hundreds of tiny people, most no larger than my hand,

moved within the circle. Many were dancing in rings—frenetic dances of stomps and spins and shouts. Others milled about, sipping a beverage from cups made of tiny blossoms. Still more people fluttered on tiny insect wings, zipping after one another in a confused game.

I turned to go, having no desire to get entangled with whatever these were.

But just as I lifted my foot over the mushroom ring, one of the tiny people called out, "The prisoner!"

I froze.

"Oh yes," giggled another. "Bring out our funny Little Thing."

The shining people did not seem to have noticed me. I breathed a sigh of relief. Then I recognized an unexpected scent, potent enough even amid the magic burn.

A human.

Several little people appeared, tugging tiny silver ropes tied around the wrists of a scrawny man in a faded orange tunic.

He stood only about my height, and his thin limbs had oversized elbows and knees. His head looked slightly too large for his body. Were all humans above ground this small? Perhaps the force of the sunlight stunted their growth.

And then, like a punch to the gut, I realized—this was no man. It was a human child.

His black skin glinted with the golden light of the shining people. The hair on his head was matted into uneven locks, with sticks and dried flowers braided through them.

For a second, his eyes met mine across the fairy ring. They were the deepest brown I had ever seen. He didn't seem to see me —he just stared ahead, his eyes empty and haunted.

Something deep inside me stirred. *This is wrong. He doesn't belong to them.* But I had my own problems to worry about. I turned to leave.

"Dance for us, Little Thing," one of the tiny people cried out.

The boy obeyed, his feet shuffling mechanically. Some of the fluttering people grabbed onto the ropes that bound his wrists and jerked him around like a puppet. He stumbled and fell to his knees, his face still blank.

The people laughed. A couple of them walked up to him and threw their tiny drinks in his face.

"Hey," I shouted.

The assembly of tiny people turned to me, their wings bristling in warning.

What was I doing? This was a terrible idea.

I cleared my throat. "You tiny mans, you let Little Thing free." I reached into my pocket and pulled out several amethysts. "You like shiny rocks? I buy him with shiny rocks."

A handful of the shimmering people fluttered close to me, inspecting the crystals. My sinuses burned more fiercely than ever.

They muttered to themselves, eyeing me.

"We like our changeling child," a tiny green-eyed female said. "You keep your rocks."

Then she gasped in surprise, chattering something to her fellows at a speed I couldn't follow.

"What?" I asked.

The little people gestured to the Master's pin against my throat. One of them reached out and touched the metal, then recoiled as though he'd been burned.

Several more swarmed around my face now. I resisted the urge to swat them away.

It took me a moment to figure out the word they kept repeating: *iron.*

"Give us the iron," the green-eyed one demanded.

I clutched at the pin. "No." There was no way I was going to part with my miracle gift—my safety ticket back through the Dominion. "It burns you, little mans."

They giggled. "It hurts our enemies. What a treasure iron is!"

I was not going to play arms-dealer for some petty savages. "No iron. Go away."

"We'll give you Little Thing."

I stopped.

In the center of the ring the boy stared blankly, their beverage still dripping from his chin. How could he know we were bargaining for his freedom?

But the Master's pin—this was the guarantee I'd be able to work my way back to Ipktu again. I needed to thank the Bandit King for having mercy on a cruel convict and buying my freedom.

I looked at the boy once more.

A prisoner.

"I give you iron pin," I said, swallowing back tears, "you free little man?"

"Oh, yes yes yes."

I jabbed a claw at them. "You let hims go now."

The boy's winged captors tugged the ropes bound to his wrists and the child followed. The little people fluttered down and placed the ropes in my hand. Gently, I led him out of the mushroom circle. The air went dark again, and we stood in the cool forest night.

Several of the little people followed me out of the circle, glowing against the blackness. They dove toward my iron pin.

"No." I snatched it away. "You put magic on him. Take magic off, then I give."

"He's just as he was when we found him," the green-eyed female insisted, hovering right in my face. "We've done nothing to him."

I snapped my teeth at her. "I smell magic. Take it off, or I *eat* you."

The glowing people swore at me—I didn't need to understand Vindorian to pick that up. I snarled.

Scowling, the leader waved her arms in front of the boy's eyes, drawing a thread of golden light from his forehead. He blinked.

I unfastened the iron pin and tossed it into the mushroom ring. The tiny people darted after it. The pin and the people disappeared into thin air.

The boy blinked again. His deep brown eyes turned to me, trying to focus.

The silvery ropes wrapped around his wrists felt as light as air. My claw sliced through them, and the falling strands vanished before they hit the forest floor.

Grasping the boy's hand, I pulled him away from the magic people's ring. He stumbled along through the dark forest as though sleepwalking.

It was painfully slow going. About then my common sense caught up with me, entirely too late as always.

What on earth was I going to do with a human child?

10

MAKOZI

W e traveled for about twenty minutes, winding between trees. A shining white orb rose above the tree line, dimming the stars and flooding the forest with silvery light. I squinted up at it.

This must be Moon they told us about. It looks stupid.

It wasn't even a proper circle—part of it was missing. Nothing in the Topside world had any decency.

The boy pulled his hand out of mine. He regarded me in the moonlight, his brow furrowed. Whatever dulling enchantment the little people had used on him seemed to be wearing off.

"You safe now, little man," I told him. "I take you home. What name you?"

He stared and said nothing.

Did he not speak Vindorian? Or was there something more serious going on? Perhaps the glowing people had broken him beyond repair.

Of course, he might have been too young to talk. An hour ago it had never crossed my mind that humans even had children. I had no idea what I was dealing with.

He stood at about my height, but for all I knew he might still be an infant. Some creatures are up on their feet within hours of birth. Maybe I'd pushed him too hard with the vigorous walk. Perhaps even now his immature body was shutting down.

Idiot. I've killed him.

I sat him down in a sheltered place between a tree trunk and a bush. "Rest," I said. "I get you food."

He sat between two thick tree roots, still watching me.

Food. Okay. What did humans eat? I thought back to the underground farm, with its rows of stems and leaves. Ah, humans eat plants. Easy enough.

I snapped off a handful of branches from a nearby shrub and piled them at his feet.

The boy stared at them.

"Stay here." I darted a short distance away, sniffing the wind. If there were a human settlement in this forest, it should be easy to pick up the scent, even from a few miles.

Nothing. Not even the smell of hearth-fires. Of course, there were so many competing odors out here that my nose struggled to make sense of it all.

After several minutes, I went back to the spot where I'd left the boy. He sat, weaving the thin branches into a cradle-like shape. He didn't seem to have eaten any of them.

Come on, child, don't make this hard.

The boy looked up at me. "Makozi Ibenwo," he said in a clear voice.

I jumped back. So he *could* talk. "What you say?"

"Makozi Ibenwo."

"What that mean?"

"My name. You asked."

Oh, I had. And he did speak Vindorian. That would help a lot.

"Yes. You name is ... Muh, uh, Kozi?"

He snickered.

Whatever, close enough. "Okay. How old you, Kozi?"

"Five."

Five months, then. Though for humans it could be years. Not that it would help me figure out which life stage he was in.

"In Hope Moon, then I'll be six," the boy added brightly. "Mama will give me a new tunic."

I glanced at his threadbare orange rags, the golden circles and triangles almost impossible to see beneath the dirt. Seemed like a change of clothes was long overdue.

"*And* a yam cake. And maybe a hat," he said. "I hope it's red. Or—"

I cut him off. "Where is you mama?"

At this the boy startled, turning around as though he'd expected her to be right behind him.

"Mama?" His lip trembled. "Mama?"

"Oh, please no cry," I pleaded.

His brown eyes brimmed with tears. "Am I lost? Am I alone?"

"No, I with you. I find you mama. How she look?"

"She ... she has hair." He sniffled.

"*Hair*? I not know *hair*."

He pointed to his mass of tangled locks.

"Oh, I know *hair*. How else she look?"

"She has ... pretty eyes. And she's really tall. And she's so, so nice." A tear slid down his cheek, and I doubted I could get any other information out of him without reducing him to a sniveling mess.

I patted his hand, awkwardly. "It fine. I find her."

Okay: hair, eyes, tall, nice. Great. That description matched literally any human adult in existence. I sighed. My best bet was to get him back to his village and let them sort it out.

"Kozi, where you live?"

The boy straightened. "I live in West Feather *nuh-ruh*, on Soldier Street, number seven." The words were crisp and practiced.

I blinked. Seven soldiers? What on earth was he talking about?

"It's the blue one," he added.

"A ... blue soldier?" I was clearly missing something.

"No, silly, a blue house."

Oh. He was reciting an address. That could be helpful, I supposed. "Good. Kozi take me to mans-town, we find you house."

A pause.

"Kozi, which way mans-town?"

"That way." He pointed toward a path snaking through a grove of gnarled trees.

Okay. Simple enough.

"Maybe it's surely that way." Makozi pointed toward a shrubby hill in the other direction. "Or that way."

"Kozi ... how well you know?"

"It's the way with so much trees."

Seriously?

"Next to the river."

"What river?" I asked.

"The blue one."

I massaged my face with my palms. Sighing, I rose to my feet. "I right back."

A few minutes later, my nose burned as I stood in front of the Wood Elf's tree. I dug my claws into its bark and tore a section away.

A branch whipped down and smacked my arm. I pushed it away and ripped off another chunk of bark.

This time the small woman appeared, her leafy hair rustling.

"You again. What gives you the right to—?"

"Where mans-town?" I demanded.

She stopped, glaring at me. "What are you talking about, you green pest?"

"You say, 'Go away from Wood Shed.' I want to go mans-town. Where I find?"

She raised an eyebrow. "What business have you with humans?"

"No matter. Where mans-town? On blue river?"

The Wood Elf crossed her arms, a smirk playing on her lips. "For your information, the closest human settlement is thirty miles from here."

It took a moment for that number to sink in. "*What*?"

Thirty miles? That would take days to walk—and that was at my pace, not with a human child in tow. What had I gotten myself into?

"You'd better get started," the Wood Elf said. "I don't want to see your face again." She vanished back into her tree with a laugh.

Resisting the urge to kick the tree trunk, I trudged back to Makozi.

The boy sat hunched over, doodling in the soil with one of the sticks I'd given him. He looked up as I approached. "I'm hungry."

I pointed at the pile of sticks that he'd left untouched.

"You food right there."

"Sticks?" His voice raised an octave. "I don't want sticks. I want food."

"But mans eat plants," I offered weakly. This was getting more complicated by the minute.

"I don't want sticks!" He let out a wail—a sound so strident I covered my ears. Goblin children never dare make that kind of racket. They only whimper, as though they know their parents won't put up with anything more. But this boy had no fear of filling the whole forest with his crying.

Panicking, I grabbed his hand. "No cry—I get you anything you want. You tell me what food it is, I find."

He sniffled, regarding me with teary eyes. "Can I have some *nuh-ruh-ruh*?"

"What?"

He repeated the unfamiliar word, wiping his nose with the back of his hand. "It's a circle you can eat. It's squishy."

This confused me even more.

He pointed at a bush some distance behind me. "Like those."

Hurrying over to the shrub, I found it laden with small soft spheres in a deep blue. They gave off an intense floral scent.

Makozi followed close behind me, snatching the spheres from my hand and gobbling them down.

Poor child *was* hungry.

I tasted a sphere and spat it out. It was cloyingly sweet—clearly not fit for eating. But it seemed to be acceptable food for humans.

At least I hoped.

Makozi moved onto the bush itself, eating spheres by the fistful. "What's your name?" he asked between swallows.

I hesitated. "Valshara Sh'a."

"Nope." He popped another sphere into his mouth. "I'll call you Magma."

"*Mag-ma*? What mean *Mag-ma*?"

"I don't know. It's just stuck up in my head." He busied himself again with eating, and I sat on a stone, waiting for him to finish.

Thirty miles. And that was assuming we could even *find* this village. I could be wandering for weeks with this boy in tow.

How was I supposed to keep this child safe when I wasn't even sure how to keep him alive? Never mind that I hadn't fully figured out how to keep myself alive in this baffling Topside world.

His mother had to be around here somewhere. And the sooner I found her, the better.

We'd just have to find this nondescript human woman in this giant enchanted forest with magical hazards around every corner.

Couldn't get much harder than that, huh?

At that moment the stone I sat upon buzzed, pulsing with a vibration that rattled my bones.

Grmm grmm GRMMMM.

I shot to my feet. It couldn't be.

Flinching, I placed my hand on the stone again. The pattern of the vibration was unmistakable.

Grmm grmm GRMMMM.

It was as though the world dropped open beneath my feet. Only one creature was powerful enough to send tremors through the stones that way.

A Blindwyrm.

11

THE BLINDWYRM

The Faceless had found my trail. With a Blindwyrm.

How did he even get access to such a monster? A Guidelight privilege?

I was as good as a Pit slave again. It didn't matter that I'd made most of my journey through water. A Blindwyrm's tongue can detect scents one thousand times better than any goblin. And the scent it had latched onto was mine.

The stone pulsed with the buzzing pattern again. I wasn't sure how exactly pushing vibrations though the stone helped the Blindwyrm find its quarry. I only knew it worked. With frightening efficiency.

Breathe, Valshara. The Faceless hasn't found you yet.

The wyrm's searching beacon could reverberate for miles. Perhaps the Faceless and his monster were still a long way underground, and it hadn't found the exit to the surface world yet.

Besides, the mouth of the cave was more like a hole. It wasn't large enough for a creature of that size.

I might have a little lead time. If I could only—

Somewhere in the darkness, a rock crashed to the ground, the sound echoing in the distance. The ground trembled beneath my feet.

The Blindwyrm was breaking through to the aboveground world.

Makozi scrambled from the bush, reaching out for my hand. "What's that noise?"

For a split second I considered leaving him behind. The wyrm wasn't after *him*. But his deep brown eyes were so wide, so intently locked onto my face.

I grabbed his hand and we ran.

My heart pounded in my ears as I heard another rock crash behind us. Perhaps we had a few minutes before the creature was on my tail.

"Kozi," I panted. "This way."

An ancient tree stood ahead, reeking of decay. I slid feet-first toward a dark hole at its base.

My knees skidded through the jagged opening, slipping over roots and soil. I landed on a floor covered in dried grass.

An animal den, based on the musky odor. Unoccupied, I hoped.

I reached out of the opening to take Makozi's hand. He drew back, looking nervously at the dark entrance.

"Kozi," I whispered, trying to sound excited. "I find magic glow bugs."

"What?"

"Yes, but be quiet so you no scare."

He let me guide his legs into the root-tangled tunnel and into the tiny chamber below. Grabbing a handful of the dried grass from the floor, I shoved it into the entrance, trying to block the opening as much as possible.

The dirt chamber was so small that Makozi had to sit on my lap. The boy was just about my size, and I grunted under his weight. He leaned his itchy hair against my chin, and I could feel his heart hammering in his chest.

"Shhh," I whispered. "Look—glow bugs."

I held up my hand and willed my fingers to shine.

Makozi gasped in surprise.

I extinguished the light. "Shh. Glow bugs hate sounds. Must stay quiet-quiet. Can you do?"

He nodded, his hair tickling my throat.

The red dots reappeared, dancing against the den ceiling. I wiggled my fingers in every pattern I could imagine, and the boy watched, transfixed.

My hands trembled. Would this hiding spot really work? The scents of rotting wood and animal musk and sweaty human overpowered my nose, but would they deter a Blindwyrm?

And it might be able to hear us breathing. Or even our hearts beating. Wyrms could detect sounds that don't even register in a goblin's ear.

Makozi, to his credit, stayed silent, watching my light show. His breathing grew slower and more regular, and after several minutes his head tilted back and lay on my chest.

Asleep.

I extinguished my light and waited.

And waited. I strained to listen over the chirps and croaks of the night creatures.

Where was it? Had the wyrm broken through the cave mouth yet? When I entered the forest, I'd been overconfident that I'd lost my pursuer and, like an idiot, had made no attempts to cover my tracks. Worse, I'd been wandering around in circles all night instead of putting any distance between me and the cavern.

Of course, if I'd just run from the mouth of the cave I'd never have rescued Makozi.

That thought brought a wave of conflicting emotions. If I had suspected what hunted me, would I have just ignored Makozi's plight? Having this boy with me put us both in more danger than if we'd stayed apart. Was it good or bad that I hadn't known about—?

The chirps and rattles stopped abruptly, and for a second the forest was silent.

Then a *pop* of a large branch cracking. It was followed by another loud crack. A tree bough crashed to the ground.

I held my breath and wrapped my arms tighter around Makozi's sleeping form.

Please, please don't wake the child.

I shrank against the earthen walls of the den, and my back came in contact with a stone lodged in the soil.

GRRRM GRRRRRM GRRRRRRMMM.

My whole body vibrated. I pulled away from the stone as fast as I dared, in case it could somehow sense me through rock.

Craning my neck, I looked out of the grass-obscured entrance. All I could see was a small patch of stars.

The stars went out.

A shadow fell across the mouth of the den, and something flickered. A forked tongue, twice as long as my arm. The tongue flicked in and out of a scaled snout, testing the scents in the air.

Searching for me.

The Blindwyrm paused and tilted its black head. For a second I caught sight of its six coal-colored horns, saw the blank indentation where its eye should have been.

Terror paralyzed me as the tongue practically entered the den entrance, flicking with new intensity. A curved fang the size of a dagger glinted in the moonlight.

It was at that moment Makozi shifted in his sleep and let out a loud sigh.

My heart stopped.

But the tongue ceased flicking. The giant snout tilted doubtfully for a moment.

Seconds felt like hours.

The tongue retreated back into the creature's mouth, and the fang flashed once more as it moved past the den entrance.

Branches crackled and the earth trembled. A wall of onyx scales undulated slowly past my window. It took a full minute for Blindwyrm's legless body to pass by, crushing the earth beneath it as it moved.

I held my breath until the sounds of rocks and branches

breaking was far in the distance and the night-insects resumed their rattling.

I don't know what it was about Makozi's sigh that had thrown the monster off my trail. Perhaps it had been trying to determine what was down in this hole and heard a noise that was definitely not goblin. Maybe even in its animal brain it knew a child would never feel safe enough to sleep near a vicious Blood Hand.

All I did know was that in my darkest moment, this boy had saved my life, just by being a child.

And in that humble little den, I clutched him in my arms for the rest of the night.

12

RAINS FALL

W hen I awoke, the child was gone.

I leapt to my feet, hitting my head on the earthen ceiling of the den. Had some Topside creature dragged him out and eaten him?

Scrambling out of the entrance, I squinted in the daylight at the thick stand of trees before me. He was nowhere to be seen.

"Kozi?" I called, hardly breathing.

Something landed behind me with a *thud*. I spun around. There was Makozi, crouching on the ground, a little cloud of dust rising around him.

Unhurt. Tension left my shoulders in a wave. "Kozi, what you do?"

"Jumping out of trees."

"Why?"

"I don't know why." He laughed, then scrambled up the closest tree. A few seconds later he hit the ground again, giggling. "Wheee!"

The behavior seemed pointless for survival, but then again I didn't know anything about humans. Sighing, I glanced toward my aching feet.

A chill ran down my spine. I stood in a rounded trough of compressed soil more than two feet wide.

The Blindwyrm's trail. The furrow traveled in an undulating pattern over the forest floor, only inches from the den where we'd been hiding. The indentation and trail of crushed plants wove off into the distance and out of sight.

Some of the broken tree branches dangled from boughs at least six feet in the air.

My red fingers trembled as I reached down to touch a stone. I could just make out the faint *grrrrrm* pattern.

The Blindwyrm was at least a few miles away, for now. I had yet to see signs of his Faceless master, but my guess was he wasn't far behind his hunting beast.

Safe, temporarily. Now what? It was day, but the sky was grey and dimmed, and the light was almost bearable.

Thud. Makozi landed beside me. "Are we gonna find my mama today?"

Might as well start now. "Yes. Come, Kozi."

Makozi skipped three steps toward the woods, then stopped. "But I'm *hun*gry."

I sighed. "Stay here." I collected a pile of the squishy orbs —*bloob berries*, Makozi called them—and laid them before him. He shoved them into his mouth, juice running down his chin.

I climbed a tree, sniffing the air. A turmoil of overpowering odors met me, most of them unrecognizable.

How was I going to sniff out a single human in this labyrinth of vegetation, all while trying to evade the Dominion's most terrifying hunter?

"Hey." Makozi pounded on the trunk of the tree I'd perched in. "Hey, Magma!"

"Kozi, quiet voice." I hissed. Did he *have* to shout?

"I finded a bug," he continued, just as loudly. "Look at this bug! Why is this a bug?"

All right, change that. Exactly how was I supposed to sniff out one human, evade a predator, *and* keep this chaotic child alive?

I slid down the trunk to where he stood. "Quiet voice, Kozi. Eat you foods."

He returned to his pile of bloob berries. A large beetle crawled over my hand and I popped it into my mouth. Not a great breakfast, but I didn't exactly have time to go foraging.

"All done."

"Good. We go."

Makozi scampered up to the tree I leaned against. "Hey, where is my little friend Beetlebuggy?"

I swallowed guiltily. "Beetle?"

"Yes. My friend." His bottom lip started to quiver.

"Oh. Well, Beetlebuggies like to fly. Maybe he flied away?"

"Then it's my job to find him," Makozi said. "Come on, Magma."

And off we went through the forest.

For the record, human children do *not* walk. They run, they climb, they skip, they wander off, and they look under every log.

After an agonizing hour, we'd barely covered half a mile.

"Look at this." Makozi twirled himself around a sapling and plucked off a large seed pod. He tapped it with his knuckle. "Anybody home? Beetlebuggy, are you in there?"

"Kozi, *please*. Hurry so we find you mama."

"Not home." He sighed and tossed the seed over his shoulder. "Oh, look—a sleeping tree." Makozi scrambled up a fallen tree trunk and pointed to its mossy bark. "See, that's his nose and his eyes. Only he has three eyes. Why does he have three eyes? Oh—Beetlebuggy, it's you—no, wait, that's not him, it's a different bug. I can tell."

I dug my claws into my palms, trying to keep my voice calm. "Please, Kozi. Just come."

"But I'm *tired*." He slid off the log and dramatically collapsed in a heap. "My legs are so hurtable. Can you carry me?"

"Carry you? Kozi, you are my same size—I not can lift you. Walk."

Makozi moaned as though in great pain, but stopped abruptly

when a dragonfly zuzzed by. He leapt to his feet and chased it down the path.

You've got to be kidding.

Two minutes later he stopped in his tracks, panic on his face. "Magma, I have to *go.*"

I rolled my eyes. "You goed two times."

"I have to go again. *Now.*"

"Fine. Go behind bush."

We couldn't keep stopping like this. Also, why did I have to be involved in this function?

A moment later, a voice came from behind the shrub. "Uh-oh."

I learned an important lesson that morning: human children *cannot* subsist on a diet of bloob berries alone.

Great. So I didn't know what else he could eat, and he wasn't exactly a reliable source of information. With every hour, it grew painfully obvious that I was not qualified to care for this child.

Out of nowhere, a dribble of water slid down my back.

I leapt to my feet. A second later, another drop hit the point of my ear, and another my nose. "What happening?"

Makozi laughed. "It's just rain, Magma."

"*Rain*? I not know *rain.*"

So apparently when you're Topside, water sometimes just falls out of the sky, drenching everything beneath it. I hated this world.

Rainwater soaked into the forest soil as we trudged along, turning it into a slick and pungent mud. Whose idea was this *rain* business anyway?

"My feet are all cold and hurted." Makozi moaned. "I wanna go home."

What do you think I've been trying to do all morning?

Beneath my stiff Master's cloak, I was soaked and miserable myself. It seemed we had no choice but to find shelter and wait this whole stupid rain thing out. It could last, what, an hour at most?

I was getting ready to settle for the roots of a wet tree when I spied a huge boulder up ahead, an inviting dark space beneath it.

"This way, Kozi."

He sniffled and followed me, his bare feet caked in mud.

As we drew closer, I realized it wasn't exactly a cave. An enormous slab of stone lay on a diagonal—one end sunk into the ground, and the other propped up by another rock. The fallen slab created a dark, sheltered space underneath, partially hidden by trees and shrubs.

"Come, Kozi. I find dry place."

I grasped his hand and pulled him toward the stone lean-to. On the way, we passed by another unusually large boulder—a towering stone rectangle, flat on either side.

As we stepped beside it, I caught that acrid whiff of magic. I paused, sniffing the air. As best I could tell, the magic was limited to the rock itself. Probably some obnoxious elf lived inside it.

I led Makozi away from the monolith and toward the fallen stone, which was also flat and rectangular. We sidled into the little dry space beneath it, and I was surprised at how roomy it was. It was big enough for a goblin and a human child to lie down in, and at the tallest point, it was even high enough for us to stand. The earthen floor was mostly dry, and I set to work clearing away a pile of round seeds that lay scattered all over it.

Then we sat and watched a new burst of rain soak the forest and drip from the edge of the stone slab above us.

The shelter was watertight. I breathed a sigh of relief.

I reached up to touch the stone roof. No Blindwyrm vibrations, but I did get a little hint of the magic smell.

"No touch rock, Kozi."

Makozi nodded. Then he sniffled again, tears brimming in his brown eyes. The poor boy looked pitiful, his thin orange tunic soaked and clinging to his thin frame.

I pulled off my red Master's cloak and wrapped it around him. The outside was wet but the inside was dry enough, and Mazoki stopped shivering.

Hugging my arms around my wet linen clothes, I waited for the rain to end.

13

RING OF STONES

I must have dozed off, because I was awakened to a loud crack.

Makozi held a rock in the air, smashing it down on one of the hard round seeds. The shell cracked, and he picked out the light-colored meat and popped it in his mouth.

"Kozi, what you eat?"

"Hazelnuts, Magma."

"They no poison you?"

"Mama said we could eat them."

Hopefully his mother had taught him correctly.

The rounded seeds appeared to have fallen from a tree right outside the shelter, so he'd have plenty to eat for now. Makozi offered a piece to me and I nearly choked on it. Not suitable food for goblins.

I stretched out my tired legs. "Kozi, when you last see you mama?"

He crunched a nut. "Last day."

"What that mean? How many day?"

He counted on his thin fingers. "I think three. Or ten."

Thanks for being so specific. So this human woman could be anywhere in the forest at this point. Doubtless searching for her child. Why hadn't we heard her calling?

"Why you come to forest if mans-town far away?"

"We went for an adventure." His expression darkened. "But Mama got lost."

"What you daddy think of advent-tour?"

"I don't have a daddy. It's naughty to ask about him."

Hmmm.

I was about to ask how he got involved with the shining people when I heard the loud crack of a falling tree.

I leapt to my feet and touched the stone ceiling.

GRRRRRRRRRRMMM.

Another cracking tree. I shoved Makozi toward the shrubs at the back of the shelter, behind the rock supporting the stone roof.

"Hey—"

"Shhh." I flattened myself against the ground and peered around the support stone.

There.

Just beyond the rectangular boulder, the Blindwyrm curled between the trees. I could see the horned head with its curved fangs and the small dark divots where eyes should have been. Its black, serpentine body stretched about twenty feet, winding between tree trunks and crushed saplings.

Its forked tongue flickered wildly, following the muddy path Makozi and I had just travelled.

Idiot me—I'd left goblin-shaped footprints.

The Blindwyrm moved closer, its tongue almost touching the rectangular boulder. Its black nostrils pulsed.

A black shadow appeared from behind a tree. The Faceless himself.

"Oh, Magma, my rock!"

Makozi's shout cut through me like a knife. I sprang up and clapped my clawed hand over his mouth, snarling at him. His eyes widened in surprise.

I held my hand over his mouth, trembling as I waited for the end.

A minute passed, then another.

I released Makozi, and he shrank further into the back of the shelter. I peered around the support stone.

The Blindwyrm had its horned head close to the muddy ground, retracing my path with its tongue working at double speed. It came up to the towering boulder we passed on the way in, its snout right at the opening.

Then the eyeless head turned away.

The Faceless stood beside the monolith. With his all-black clothing I couldn't tell if he was facing me or looking back into the woods.

He crouched and studied the mud—yes, I'd left obvious prints. His gloved fingers traced them to the boulder, and then he stopped, shaking his head in frustration.

They acted as though my trail had led right into a wall.

I let my eyes wander around the woods. A few yards away from the rectangular boulder stood another huge stone slab, half-hidden behind a tree. Beyond that was another monolithic stone, then another.

A ring.

The giant stones were in a ring. This shelter was part of it—a fallen monolith that still kept the circle unbroken.

I thought back to the shining people's ring of mushrooms. I'd been standing right beside it, but couldn't see the people's light or hear their drunken songs until I stepped inside.

Rings meant something in Woodshea. They protected whoever was within, masking them from outside perception. That's why I smelled magic in the stones.

As long as we stayed inside the circle of monoliths, the Faceless couldn't see or hear us. His Blindwyrm couldn't smell us, and it couldn't detect us with its vibrations. As far as anyone who meant us harm was concerned, the stones around us formed an impassible wall.

I sat up a little straighter, breathing thanks for this latest miracle of my new life.

The Faceless and the wyrm retraced my path several more

times, then withdrew into the forest. I had a feeling they wouldn't be gone long.

I turned to the back of the shelter to find Makozi huddled in the corner, tears streaming down his face.

Had he seen the Blindwyrm? Is that what had frightened him so? I reached my hand toward him, and he drew back.

"Kozi?"

His lip trembled. "I just—I just wanted to tell you I lost my rock."

It took me a moment to figure out what he was talking about. Makozi had yelled something about a rock when I was watching our hunters. I'd clapped my hand over his mouth to stop him from getting us killed.

Well, if he was upset about me trying to save our lives, he could just get over that. Let him be a little scared of me. That's how my parents raised me.

But then I saw his sad brown eyes and my heart melted.

"Hey," I said softly. I found his rock on the earthen floor and held it out to him.

Makozi hesitated, then stretched his hand toward me. I placed the rock in his palm and scooted beside him.

He looked away.

"Hey," I said again. "Kozi, I not mean to scare you. I very regret."

The boy sniffled and said nothing.

I sighed. "I regret very much. Magma ... Magma not good with childs."

"You sometimes are," Makozi mumbled, wiping his nose on my red cloak.

I put my hand on his shoulder. "Kozi is good child, kind child. Magma not mean to be rough. I was scared by you loud sound."

"Magma's afeared of noise?"

I paused. It was unfair to hide from him the dangers that followed us. But I had the feeling if he knew, it would only frighten him. I myself was scared out of my mind, and I was ex-military. He was just a child.

"Yes," I said. "Sometimes noise very, very scary for Magma. But I too rough. I very regret."

He snuggled into my shoulder. "It's all right."

I put my arm around him, both grateful and unsettled by his ready forgiveness. I had a feeling that even if I continued to be hard on him, he'd still cling to me, perhaps even blaming himself for my overreactions.

For the time being, I was responsible to keep him safe—from the monsters behind us, and from my own carelessness. It was a ponderous burden.

"Kozi," I said, "What if we have code?"

Makozi perked up. "What kind of code?"

"Well, when Magma is scared of noise, and needs quiet, I say special word. Then you be serious quiet."

"What will the word be?"

"Any word Kozi likes."

He thought for a minute, then grinned. "What about *burps*?"

"Sure, Kozi. *Burps*."

14

STICKS THAT SWIM

The Blindwyrm returned the next morning before Makozi awoke. Even my path going cold wasn't enough to deter the Faceless from his hunt.

Makozi and I were safe inside the stone ring, but we were also trapped. I watched the Faceless kick at the rectangular boulder in frustration, finally leading the Blindwyrm away.

Wandering around the forest looking for Makozi's mother was not an option.

Trying to make a thirty-mile trek to the nearest human settlement was not an option.

Staying in this circle with nothing but a dwindling supply of hazelnuts and a few beetles was not an option.

I'd run out of options.

Makozi seemed content with his breakfast of nuts for now, but hunger was starting to compromise my ability to think.

I sat in the drizzling rain, wrapping large leaves over my feet and binding them with strands of grass.

Makozi looked up from his game—something that involved throwing sticks into puddles. "What're you doing?"

I pulled a makeshift lace tighter. "I make shoes."

"Why do they look stupid?"

"Because Magma bad at shoes. Kozi, listen. You stay in stone circle." I pointed to the border of stones. "I no want you get lost. I right back. I find you bloob berries."

I took a breath and stepped outside the circle. Hopefully the improvised shoes would not only distort my footprints, but prevent my scent from being left in the soil.

That was probably wishful thinking, so I did my best to walk through puddles and rivulets of water.

I managed to find a few of those jumping amphibians and several mushrooms—as well as the promised berries.

Venturing a few more yards, I nearly stumbled into rushing water. A narrow river flowed right through the heart of the forest, scattered boulders creating whitewater caps.

I felt a stir of hope. Didn't Makozi say his town was beside a river?

It wasn't necessarily the same one—for all I knew, Topside could have more than one river. And this one looked swift and deep. Swimming it would be difficult for me, and certainly impossible for the boy.

I hurried back to the safety of the stone ring. Makozi sat in the shelter, braiding strands of grass and tying twigs together.

Whatever keeps you busy.

I sat for a while in the shelter, eating my last amphibian and watching the rain that had started up again. I hoped it washed away any trace of my scent outside the ring.

Makozi darted out into the rain with his little bundle of sticks. He ran to a mud-puddle and made a great show of pushing the sticks into the water. After a few minutes of blowing at the sticks, he entertained himself by stomping his bare foot in the puddle to make waves.

I would never understand this child.

"Kozi," I called. "Eat you berries."

Makozi hopped over to me, grinning as raindrops soaked his matted hair.

I piled up the bloob berries and reached for the Bandit King's mug, which I'd left sitting in the rain to collect water.

"To drink," I told him, seconds before he grabbed one of his tiny twigs and dropped it inside.

Sigh.

He picked up the mug and swirled the water around, giggling as the tiny piece of wood struggled in a whirlpool. When the water calmed, the twig bobbed back to the surface.

Wait—had I seen that right?

"Kozi? Why tiny tree not sink?"

He laughed. "Wood swims, Magma. Didn't you know that?"

"Uh ... no?" How would I know that random piece of Topside knowledge?

I glanced over to his puddle. His little bundle of sticks drifted on the muddy surface.

"I'm making boats," Makozi said proudly.

"*Boats?*"

He picked up one of his tied-together stick bundles. "The man sits here." He pointed to a spot on the top. "And the boat swims down the river, and he gets all the way to the market. Probably with peaches."

A wheel started turning in my head. "Kozi, do big wood float?"

"Sure."

"And ... if we got big wood, and tied together, could Magma and Kozi sit on top while boat swims?"

His eyes lit up. "We could make a *big* boat?"

"Yes, big. Maybe we could swim on river to mans-town?"

He sprang to his feet. "All the way to Soldier Street!"

This might work, provided I'd found the right river, and that Makozi knew how to scale up his boat design, and that we didn't drown in the process.

We might need a miracle or two, but this could provide an escape from the Blindwyrm and get Makozi home.

I stood. "Kozi, you get grass for make ropes. I go find woods."

I didn't have to stray far out of the circle to find wood large enough. Our friend the Blindwyrm had snapped several boughs cleanly from their trees and left them strewn all along the path. I dragged seven or eight back into the safety of the ring, wondering what the Faceless would make of those marks in the mud.

I hoped this wasn't a mistake.

When I'd piled the boughs up, I spotted Makozi in the arms of a tree. I scowled. "Why you not get grass?"

He waved something long and green at me. "Look, Magma, I finded vines all over these trees."

"*Vines*?"

"They're like tree-ropes. Better than grass." He tossed one down to me, and I caught it. The leafy stem was long and flexible, and surprisingly strong. A few of these braided together would make a very sturdy binding for our boat.

"You smart one, Kozi."

Beaming, he dropped another piece of vine at my feet.

We worked through the rest of the morning, paying little attention to the drizzle. Makozi brought me his model boats—apparently he was mimicking several styles of actual watercraft he'd seen in his hometown. We picked the simplest one, a rectangular raft of logs fastened together with rope.

The raft would have to be narrow and lightweight, since the two of us would need to carry it, not drag it, when it was time. Leaving boat-shaped marks in the mud leading straight to the river would be a dead giveaway to the Faceless. Better to leave a set of ambiguous footprints that just stopped at the river shore.

I had almost finished the last knots on the binding when Makozi cried out in pain.

"Magma!" He pulled his finger away from a splintered piece of bough and grasped it. "Ow—it hurts, it's too hurtable."

I grasped his hand and examined his finger, relieved to find there was no blood drawn. "You fine, Kozi."

But the panic in his voice didn't subside. "It *hurts*, Magma. I need you to *nuh-ruh*."

"To what?"

"To *nuh-ruh* it." Again I missed the word, and he took to demonstrating the action.

I cocked my head. "You want me put my lips on it and make a smacking sound?"

He nodded through tears.

I hesitated, not seeing how this would do any good. Drawing his hand toward my face, I pressed my lips against his uninjured finger. "Mwah?"

He sighed. "Thank you, Magma." He then went back to work on the raft, as content as ever.

I sat back, wondering about this latest miracle in my new life. Somehow, without my noticing it, my saliva had gained the power to heal.

THE RAIN SUBSIDED LATE that afternoon. Makozi ate up the rest of the fallen hazelnuts and we took turns drinking rainwater from the Bandit King's cup. I learned the hard way that you should always drink *before* handing the cup to a child.

Breathing a word of thanks for our ring shelter, I turned to Makozi and put my hand on his shoulder. "Ready?"

He grinned and put his hand on *my* shoulder. We were about the same height, after all.

Makozi and I lifted the raft above our heads and bent forward so the weight rested on our upper backs.

I pointed us toward a gap between a tree and one of our protecting stones.

"No forget, Kozi. *Burps.*"

The boy giggled, but kept quiet as we carried the raft through the woods.

With every step, my leaf-shod feet sank a few inches into the muddy forest floor. Makozi, as instructed, made sure to step into the prints I made.

I hadn't told him it was to help cover my scent.

The trip to the river shore took fewer than ten minutes, and I held my breath for most of it, straining my ears for the noise of breaking tree boughs. The only sound I heard was the rush of water over stones.

We found a shallow part of the river bank and lowered the raft to the water's edge. The front ends of the logs bobbed in the current, as though eager to start the journey.

I swallowed. "Kozi, come," I whispered.

The boy was gone. After a tense moment, he reappeared, wrestling a long tree branch out of the woods.

This child and his sticks.

I pointed to the raft, urgently. The longer we stood, the more danger we were in. Makozi leapt on top of the raft, his new stick clattering against the uneven logs. I winced.

I put my hands on the back of the raft, preparing to push off the bank. The river's whitecaps looked more intimidating than ever.

"Kozi," I asked, "You sure this not kill us?"

"Yep, so sure."

He was the expert. I gave the raft a shove and jumped onto its uneven surface as the current grabbed hold of it.

The boughs wobbled and lurched beneath our feet, and I fought to keep my balance. I looked ahead to see a line of white waves, sharp rocks barely peeking out above the surface.

"Magma?"

"What?"

"What's a 'killus'?"

But there was no time to answer. The front of the raft tipped upward as we hit the first rapid. The next second it plunged toward the water. White water surged over the top of the raft, soaking us to our knees.

Well, I guess this is how I die.

A moment later the water drained away through the gaps between logs. The raft rose back to the top of the water, just as Makozi had promised it would.

I stumbled toward the child and clutched his arm. He seemed unfazed by the rocking movement of the raft beneath him. In fact, he looked like he was having fun.

Before I could catch my breath, we went over a second set of rapids. The raft tilted and veered off toward the left, heading right for a huge rock.

Without missing a beat, Makozi picked up his tree bough and pinned the end against the rock. The branch jammed back toward him and nearly knocked him off his feet.

I scrambled toward the boy and wrapped my arms around him, bracing us against the force of the bough. Together we managed to push the raft away from the rocks.

We had little time to celebrate, though—the craft raced toward another set of treacherous rapids. But with our combined strength and Makozi's keen ability to aim the bough at just the right time, we got through without being smashed.

Eventually the river quieted, growing wider and less rocky. The raft floated along in the current, bobbing gently.

I flopped down onto the wet logs, exhausted. Makozi sat beside me, leaning his head on my shoulder. I patted his tangled locks.

"Good boy, Kozi. The best boy."

He puffed out his chest a little. "I am an expert of boats."

We sat in silence for several minutes, enjoying a hard-earned rest. I watched the dense tree line on either side of the river. No sign of a huge black serpent.

"Magma?" Makozi lifted his head from my shoulder and peered into my face. "Are you a fairy?"

"*Fairy*? I not know *fairy*."

"They're like little magic people. Mama says they glow."

I frowned. "Kozi, little shining mans—are they fairy?"

He shrugged. "I never saw one. Mama said to watch for them when we got to the forest. She wanted to find them."

Never saw one? I pressed a little deeper. "You never see little shining mans that dance?"

Confusion clouded over his face for a just a moment, then he shrugged again. "I don't think so."

Apparently when his tiny captors had removed their spell from Makozi's mind, they'd also erased all memories of themselves. That was a mercy—he wouldn't have to relive the trauma of their mistreatment.

"Why you mama want a fairy?"

"To get help."

"What help?"

"I don't know what help."

So his mother had gone to Woodshea on purpose, naïve about the dangers of fairies. Is that how the shining people had gotten a hold of Makozi? Perhaps they'd tricked his mother into a bargain in which they claimed her child. Or maybe they'd just taken him while she slept.

Was she still wandering the woods, searching for him? Was I stealing her child out of her arms?

But I didn't have a choice. I'd searched as much as I'd dared, and I could no longer wander around the forest with the Blindwyrm on my tail. If I found other humans, they'd be able to help —maybe even send a search party out to find her. My job was to get this child back to the safety of his kind.

"So are you a fairy?" Makozi's question broke off my musing.

"No. I goblin."

He pondered that for a moment, and I wondered if he'd learned the same sort of prejudices about goblins that we had about humans.

"Then why are you helping?"

"Because ..." I wasn't sure how to verbalize my new and unfamiliar emotions. "Magma *want* to help Kozi."

"All day?"

"All day."

The clouds above us broke up, the light streaming through them a fiery red. I jumped to my feet. What new horror was this?

Makozi laughed. "It's just sunshine, Magma."

"Why it red?"

"The sunshine makes colors when it goes down."

Would I ever make sense of this crazy Topside world?

I sat back down on the damp wooden raft, and Makozi leaned beside me, his leaf-strewn hair tickling my face. I watched the sky change from red to purple to indigo.

Makozi sniffled, and a tear splashed onto my arm.

"Oh Kozi, what wrong?"

"I want Mama." He wiped his nose with the back of his arm and sobbed. "I miss her so, so much."

I tilted his face toward mine. "Listen, Kozi. Magma find you mama. I promise."

He nodded through his tears. "But I want her *now*."

"Ah." I pulled him close and wrapped my arm around him. Now what?

"Kozi, if you mama here right now, what she do?"

"Sing a song." He sighed. "Magma? Could *you* sing?"

I frowned. I hadn't sung a tune since I was a child myself. I closed my eyes and tapped into one of my earliest memories, to the air my mother once sang. For a moment I felt safe and secure. I stroked Makozi's tangled hair and sang,

"Ah lah ay,
Lah ay-lah lay
Ah lah ay."

He sniffled and snuggled a little closer. "What does it mean?"

"What what mean?"

"The words. What do they mean?"

"Nothing. It just singing. They just singing-words."

He yawned. "Songs should have real words to them."

Where did this child get such strange ideas?

"Don't worry, next time you can learn a better song." And a few minutes later he was asleep, his head resting on my arm like it was a pillow.

At that point the sunlight had faded altogether, and the first stars appeared. I marveled at these little pinpricks of ice, strewn unevenly across the sky in myriad patterns.

Maybe not everything about this Topside world was terrible.

My eyes grew heavy and I shook myself to fight off sleep. I studied the dark tree line along the shore, watching for movement.

And then somehow I was in the woods. In the distance stood a woman in a long red dress. She moved to and fro in a panicked manner, calling something I couldn't make out.

"Wait," I cried. "Are you looking for a child? I've found him— I've found your boy."

I ran toward her, my feet floating over the forest floor. But no matter how fast I ran or how loud I yelled, the woman in red remained just out of reach of my voice.

I startled awake. The moon had risen, looking smaller and even more squashed tonight. I splashed some cold water on my face and kept watch, Makozi curled up beside me.

And under the stars, the river carried us away from Woodshea and into a new unknown.

15

THE BUSY RIVER

Dawn rose over the river, turning the water a curious shade of pink. I closed my weary eyes, focusing my attention on a far-off sound.

Hollow knocking echoed through the woods. The pattern was erratic but purposeful, with long phrases of complicated rhythms that repeated regularly.

What was going on? I glanced down at Makozi, snoring beneath the red Master's cloak. It was a shame to wake him, but we were a team now, and I needed his insight.

I put my hand on his shoulder and shook gently. He rolled over with a sleepy smile.

"Kozi? What that noise?"

I waited for him to say something like, *Oh, Magma, don't you know about the beetles that drum on the flowers?* or *The air always makes a clacking noise in the morning,* or some other kind of nonsense that seemed to be normal up here.

Instead, he sat up straight and grinned.

"What it is?" I asked.

He leaned forward on the raft eagerly. "Home, Magma, home."

I blinked. "Soldier Street makes knocking sound?"

Makozi giggled. "No, Magma. Those are the talking drums."

Oh, of course, *talking* drums. How could I have not guessed that?

"The drums mean codes. They're hit by people. So if we hear drums, it means we're close to the people who hit them. Close to B'jeme."

"*Jem*? I not know *Jem*."

"That's the name of the place."

"What place?"

"The city."

So we were already close to the human settlement. River travel was much faster than I'd expected. We might even arrive at the city before noon. And then Makozi and I would find Soldier Street—whatever that was—reunite him with his family, and alert them that his mother might still be in the forest. They'd take care of him from there. My rescue would be complete, and Makozi and I would say goodbye.

A painful lump rose in my throat. That last idea hit me harder than I'd expected.

But I had to get the boy back to the safety of his kind. He couldn't stay with me any longer, not with the Faceless and the Blindwyrm on my tail.

Once Makozi was safe, I'd melt into the Topside world, finding new ways to evade my hunters until I could make my way back to Ipktu. It would be more complicated now without the help of the Master's pin, but I had no regrets about that trade now.

I leaned into Makozi's side and watched the forest go by, almost wishing I could slow down the current beneath us.

A quiet hour or so passed. Grey clouds rolled in above us, dimming the intense daylight. I watched the tree-lined river banks, waiting for signs of the human settlement.

"Oh!" I grabbed Makozi's arm and pointed at the huge white triangle barreling straight for us.

He patted my hand. "Don't worry. It's just a dhow."

"*Dow?* I not know—"

"A boat, Magma. A giant, big boat." Makozi leapt to his feet and waved, laughing as the raft tilted beneath us.

A moment later the dhow reached us. Its huge cloth triangle billowed with the wind, and the force of the trapped air pushed the vessel against the river current. I had to admit, that was clever.

Beneath the cloth was a smooth-sided boat, painted black and fashioned into a sleek design that cut through the water.

"Hello," Makozi called up to the dhow as our raft bobbed in its wake. "How are you? How is your sailing?"

Figures appeared over the side of the boat—fully grown men at least twice my height, their black skin glistening with sweat. I wrinkled my nose.

Instead of waving back to Makozi, they pointed and muttered something I couldn't pick up. I realized they were glaring at *me*.

They continued to watch me as their boat clipped by, exchanging frowns. For a moment I thought they were going to turn the dhow around and stop us, but the ship continued sailing up the river, leaving a trail of white water behind.

A goblin traveling alone with a human child must have looked very suspicious. Humans probably couldn't imagine me meaning a child anything but harm.

Makozi had shed the Master's cloak as the air around us had gotten warmer. I lifted it from the damp raft floor and wrapped it around myself, pulling the hood low over my head. The red fabric came only to my knees, so I couldn't do anything about my green legs and clawed feet. But it was the best I could do.

"Magma, are you cold?"

I shrugged. "Sure."

A few minutes later, another large boat passed—this one with three rectangular sails and a square wooden body. The brown-haired sailors nodded at Makozi's enthusiastic waving but hardly gave me a second glance.

The next ship had no sail, but instead an assortment of sweaty humans who dragged wooden rods through the water, fighting the current with pure strength and stubbornness. They didn't seem to even notice us.

My disguise was working.

Meanwhile, the river grew more crowded with watercraft. Navigation grew harder, and we hugged the river bank. Makozi got to work with his tree bough, pushing us away from rocks and dislodging us from shallow places.

"Kozi, why so many boats?"

"There are always lots of boats at B'jeme."

Now it made sense why he'd come up with so many different boat models. This was his world.

A moment later, the raft hit the bank and jerked to a halt, the logs riding up onto the sandy shore.

I stumbled forward. "Why we crash?"

Makozi hopped onto the sand. "We didn't crash. We *landed*."

I looked around the wooded bank and saw no sign of human habitation. "This is Soldier Street?"

He laughed. "No, silly Magma. We can't use the dock because that costs money." He had the air of an adult explaining something to a child. "So we land here and walk in."

"Okay. I get shoes." I wrapped the leaves around my feet. I was betting on us having lost our pursuers at this point, but there was no sense leaving an obvious set of footprints in the wet soil.

We left our scraggly raft behind and pushed our way through heavy foliage. For all the water traffic in the river behind us, it seemed strange that this path to the city was abandoned.

"Kozi? You sure this go to *Jem*?" I asked after several minutes of fighting through shrubs and low-hanging branches.

"Yup." He plucked a flower from its stem, studied it, and then tossed it aside.

"This not look like city path."

"Because it's secret. Just for me and Mama." He stopped and pointed. "Hey, look, B'jeme!"

16

MARKET IN THE CENTER OF THE WORLD

There, in the middle of the forest, an enormous rectangle of red mud reached toward the sky. It stretched through the forest in either direction, as far as the eye could see.

"*This* is mans-town?"

Makozi giggled. "No, Magma. That's a wall. B'jeme is inside."

I approached the huge structure—it had to be more than forty feet tall. I shoved my shoulder against its flat surface, but found the packed earth was hard and unyielding. I could dig my claws into it, but as soon as I put any weight on them, the red earth crumbled beneath my fingers.

There would be no scaling this. "How we get in?"

"Follow me."

Makozi led me along the side of the wall, heading back toward the river. This inefficient "secret path" only made sense if your goal was not to be seen.

"Kozi," I asked, "is this the way you mama came when you went to find fairies?"

"Yup. But we left at night-time."

I considered the pieces of the puzzle. Makozi didn't know his father and had learned not to ask. At some point his mother was so desperate for help—help that she couldn't get back home—

that she snuck her child out of the city at night. She set out to find the fairies, whom she knew nothing about, and they'd stolen her child from her.

Whatever all this meant, it didn't seem happy.

"Hey, what's our relevant doing here?" Makozi ran ahead, disappearing into an especially dark part of the forest. By the time I caught up with him, he was tugging a vine away from an enormous tree.

"What wrong, Kozi?"

"Someone moved our relevant." He pulled indignantly at the vine, revealing a smooth, whitish bark beneath. The tree was at least six times wider than its neighbors, and perfectly circular.

"How somebody move this giant tree, Kozi?"

"Not a tree, Magma. A statue."

"Statue of a tree?"

Makozi sighed. "Not a tree," he said with condescending patience. I recognized the tone and didn't much like it. "A relevant. This is his *leg*."

My eyes followed the white column to where it disappeared into the treetops above. Something huge blotted out the sun, but I couldn't see past the foliage. Whatever this thing was, it had been here long enough to be incorporated into the forest canopy.

I knocked against the waterlogged surface of the tree—er, leg. A chunk of yellowing plaster broke off, leaving a dark hole.

Something scurried around inside—a small creature with grimy fur and a long naked tail. I grasped Makozi's hand and pulled him away. "This statue old and gross. Come."

"Poor relevant," Makozi said as we returned to the path beside the wall. "He doesn't belong in the woods. He belongs at the city corner, to remember to us, 'strength through wisdom and jenosity.'"

"*Jenosity*?"

"It's when you have jens and you give them to people."

"Ah."

We followed the wall toward the river, and I caught whiff of overwhelming odors. I couldn't decipher most of them, but one was dominant: human sweat.

Oh, boy.

Sounds drifted toward me: voices shouting, water splashing, metal clanging. Multiple strands of music—all very different and unharmonized—played over the top of the constant clatter of wooden drums.

Loudest of all was a strange pattern of wooden creaks and metallic groans.

Makozi and I reached the corner of the city wall. The dirt path beneath us gave way to a broad surface made of wooden planks. We stepped onto it—the *boardwalk*, Makozi called it— and turned the corner.

I recoiled. On either side of the boardwalk, a monstrous contraption of wood and metal groaned, moving of its own accord.

On the left, a huge wheel rotated, its wooden spokes dipping down into the river water and rising high into the air.

On the right, flush against the city's front wall, six metal shafts bobbed up and down, dropping into giant iron cylinders and slowly rising again. With each rise, I heard a faint gurgle of water.

"Hey!" Makozi sounded offended. "That's where the relevant's supposed to be."

I pointed at the enormous contraption. "Kozi—what that is?"

He shrugged. "I don't know. I never saw it."

Again, doubt flickered through my mind. "Kozi is *sure* this is B'jeme?"

"Yep. Oh, Magma, look—the market." He grabbed my hand and pulled me past the mysterious machine.

The path ahead was swallowed up by a chaos of color and noise and movement. Cloth canopies in a dozen different patterns draped over the boardwalk, and on either side stood cluttered booths with wares spilling out onto the walkway.

Hundreds of humans milled about. I raised my red hood just in time to obscure my face.

A cloud of odors overpowered my nose. I clapped my hands over my face and tripped over a pile of root vegetables. Makozi pulled me back before I crashed into a tower of finely detailed clay urns.

"Watch it," warned a man sitting behind precarious stacks of pottery.

I nodded apologetically beneath my cloak, my senses spinning. Makozi took my hand and led me deeper into the crowd.

The place teemed with humans, most of them twice our height.

I never imagined that one species could have so much variation. Women with skin as black as Makozi's pushed by us, their long dresses adorned with colorful geometric patterns. A man with dark wavy hair struggled by, his bronze arms wrapped around a mountain of white fiber. A young woman with a beige complexion, whose blossom-covered robe was tied back with an oversized bow, haggled with a merchant selling opals. The merchant's long white locks and colorless linen clothing reminded me of the humans who lived near Ipktu, but a veil obscured his face so I couldn't be sure. I even caught sight of one man whose face was so pale it was almost white, his hair as orange as copper.

All of these humans were sweating in the heat of the marketplace, and my stomach turned with the stench.

Vendors shouted at us, and my instinct was to bolt. But Makozi walked along, ignoring them. I realized after a moment they were calling out the names of their goods.

The path ahead of us was strewn with all sorts of items: baskets overflowing with nuts and fruit; dead-eyed fish hanging from hooks; dishes piled high with a red powder that set my nostrils aflame; and globs of foul-smelling stuff that Makozi called *cheese*.

Makozi chattered in my ear, pointing at various items. "Can we get apples? Ooh, paper, I need new paper. Hey, he has swords!

Mama never lets me get a sword. Whoops, stepped on a grape—squish. Wanna see yourself in a mirror?"

I nodded, pretending I understood what he was blathering on about. Meanwhile, my chest grew tighter by the moment, suffocated by heat and odors. An urge rose up within me to scream, to flee, to flail my claws and strike at the dozens of people practically touching my body.

"Clear the way!" The boardwalk rumbled beneath our feet, and the people around us wedged themselves between sales displays.

My stomach dropped. A centaur barreled toward us, his four black hooves pounding the wooden boards. My military training had prepared me for this horrible eventuality: being crushed to death by a Kavannan warrior.

He would have trampled me, too, if Makozi hadn't yanked me out of the way. As the centaur tromped past, I noticed this "warrior" was heavy around the middle, his long black hair thinning on top of his head. A wooden cart trailed behind him, piled high with sacks of grain. As soon as he passed, the crowd flooded back into the narrow walkway.

"Kozi, I thought it was mans-town. Why is centaur come here?"

Makozi studied a basket full of red fruit. "It's the Central Market, in the center of the world. Everybody comes here."

"Centaurs?"

"Yep, and also everybody."

I tried to look calm despite the stress pumping through my body. "Can we go Soldier Street now?"

Makozi laughed. "Soldier Street is in B'jeme."

"But you said—"

"B'jeme is inside the walls. We have to go through the gate."

"*Gate*?"

"There." He pointed to a break in the vendor stalls. A set of white stairs led up to a keyhole-shaped opening in the red wall.

We climbed the steps, leaving the market behind us. I gasped for air, as though I'd escaped drowning in a flood of humanity.

On either side of the keyhole gate stood black-skinned guards, their hair in tight curls close to their heads. Both men were dressed in long robes of olive green, and they held lances topped with double-edged blades.

I looked through the opening into a city of red rectangles. A far more reasonable number of humans walked along its streets.

At last.

I approached the threshold and the men in green stopped me, their lances pointing and me and the boy.

"You—where is your *duh-ruh?*"

I cowered beneath my hood, afraid to let them see my goblin face.

"I said, where is your *duh-ruh?*"

"He says *stamp*, Magma," Makozi whispered.

"*Stamp?* I not know *stamp.*"

The men in green moved forward, forcing us back down the first stair. "No stamp, no entrance to B'jeme. That's the law."

"But this boy is lost. Hims family is so sad waiting inside."

The guard leaned closer to me, trying to see my shadowed face. "Is that so? Then where's his stamp?"

I glanced over at Makozi, who shrugged. "I don't know a stamp," he said.

The second guard scowled. "I don't know who you are, but using a child as a ploy to infiltrate our city is a new low."

Heat flushed through my face. "I not ploy. I travel so far to bring hims home."

The first guard rattled his lance. "Move along."

This couldn't be happening. After all we'd gone through, we were being turned away mere feet from Makozi's home. We descended the staircase, back toward chaos.

"Makozi, how you lose your stamp?"

"Never had one."

I paused on the stairs. "You *sure* this is you mans-town?"

"The man said it was B'jeme."

He had a point. But how could Makozi know so little about his own city?

"Hey," the guard called. "We said move along."

The boy and I took a few more steps down. "Can I see my mama now?"

"Soon. Magma need to think." My heartbeat quickened as we approached the throng of humanity below. "Kozi, can we *not* go market?"

He thought for a moment. "Let's go see the boats. This way."

17

THE DOCK INCIDENT

W e re-entered the suffocating marketplace, but only for a moment. Makozi wove between a few vendor stalls and I followed.

A moment later, we stood on a cluttered dock, the market to our backs. A river breeze rustled my red cloak. Dark clouds roiled over the treeline, threatening rain.

We managed to find a clear spot among the piles of empty sacks, broken pottery, and other debris that littered the boardwalk here.

I sat down, exhausted, and Makozi sat beside me, swinging his legs over the edge of the dock. "Have you never seen so much boats, Magma?"

He wasn't kidding. The docks stretched as far as I could see in either direction, with rickety piers reaching out into the water in uneven intervals.

The wooden posts that supported the piers were wrapped up in ropes and cables, all anchoring separate watercraft. Tiny rowboats and fishing vessels bobbed alongside black dhows and enormous ships with neat rows of oars.

As I looked out over the jumble, I realized some of the boats weren't tied to the dock at all—they were just tied to the closest ship.

Out of the stormy sky, a heavy breeze took up, fluttering a hundred idle sails. Some of the ships thudded against the wood of the piers. The humans darting in and out of the vessels didn't seem to notice, too busy carrying pots and baskets of goods to and from the market.

Out on the open river, more watercraft passed by. Some came within mere feet of tied-up vessels, tossing the smaller ones around in their wake.

I didn't know much about shipyards, but this whole mess looked like a disaster waiting to happen.

Makozi busied himself by trying to teach me all the names of the different boat styles and how they were propelled.

My mind was elsewhere, though. What were we going to do now? If we were ever going to reunite Makozi with his family, I had to get him into that city. But those unclimbable walls had only one entrance, and it was guarded.

The best thing to do, then, was to wait until nightfall and kill the guards. Those lances wouldn't work well at close proximity, and I was fairly certain that in cover of darkness I could leap onto the first guard's neck before ...

Revulsion swept over me in an unexpected wave. Even in my imagination I couldn't finish the deed. What two weeks ago would have been a logical strategy—and a task that would have fired me up—had suddenly become a horror.

I glanced over at my chattering boy, a lump forming in my throat. Killing a stinking human, even for his sake, was now I line I couldn't cross.

Which at the moment was extremely unhelpful. I shifted my weight and one of the amethysts in my pocket dug into my thigh.

Wait a minute.

I put my hand on Makozi's shoulder, interrupting his nautical lecture, and pressed a crystal into his palm.

"Kozi, go to market. Find mans who sell stamps."

He looked at the purple stone in his dark palm and nodded. "Sure. Oh, but wait. The market's closed soon."

"*Closed*? I not know—"

Shouts rang out at the end of one of the rickety piers. "Watch out!"

A massive trade ship, its curled bowsprit trimmed with gold, barreled toward the pier. Its single sail bulged with an unexpected storm wind, and blond-haired centaurs on the deck struggled with a network of ropes meant to control it.

People on the dock scrambled out of the way. The two-story wooden hull struck a small dhow, flipping it over and pinning it against the pier.

With a crunch of wood, the gilded ship lurched to a stop.

I held tight to Makozi's hand as a crowd of humans rushed past us, shouting and helping up injured dock workers. A few nimble men climbed onto the gilded ship, scrambling up the mast and helping the centaurs disable the rogue sail.

I pulled my red cloak further down over my face. "We go," I said to Makozi. This wasn't the sort of thing a young child should dwell on.

But just as we stood to leave, I heard a high-pitched shriek.

"Teacher's still in there!"

Three girls with tightly braided hair pointed at the vessel that the gilded ship had run over. The dhow had capsized, the beams of its exposed keel distorted and partially snapped against the dock.

"He's still inside. Help!"

Several people rushed toward the little boat, pounding on the dark wood.

"Hello? Anyone there?"

One peered through a splintery fissure in the wood. "It's Old Folorunso. He's trapped."

"It's taking on water—hurry."

A man with wavy hair and baggy trousers jumped into the

water, trying to squeeze himself into the crack. "It's no use—it's too small."

A second man waved frantically at the would-be rescuer. "Get out of there—it's going down!"

The little girls screamed.

I pulled off my red cloak and handed it to Makozi. "Stay here. Do not wander. I right back, in two minutes."

I darted toward the damaged pier, weaving in between the legs of the crowd. A woman shrieked when she saw my green skin and bare head, and the cluster of rescuers drew back in surprise when I appeared.

"Where hole?" I demanded.

"W-what?" stammered a merchant in a wide-sleeved robe.

I pointed at the dhow. "Man inside, how to get in?"

One of the rescuers shook his head. "It's too small." He gave me a second glance, and raised an eyebrow. "Actually—can you fit through that?"

The breach in the keel was now halfway submerged in the churning river water. I dropped into the murky waves and managed to squeeze through the splintered crack.

The space inside the flipped dhow was dark as pitch. I shone my red light, trying to orient myself. Between the curved floor-turned-ceiling and the black water, I had less than a foot of air to work with.

A wooden bench bobbed next to me, and swaths of cloth brushed against my legs.

"Man? Where man?"

"Who's there?" came a weak voice from the corner.

In the dim red light I saw a white-haired head, just barely staying above water.

I splashed toward the figure and grabbed him by his shoulders. "I help you." But as I pulled him toward the center of the ship, his long tunic caught fast on something on the wall.

My claws slashed his clothing as the pocket of air shrank to a mere eight inches.

"Stay here," I said, as though he had a choice. I dove beneath the water, trying to discern an exit with my dim red light. Good thing I knew nothing about boats.

There.

I resurfaced and turned to the man, his eyes wide and white against his dark skin.

"Breathe. We go out."

He inhaled obediently. I pushed his head beneath the water and grabbed his hand, diving for the exit below.

After five seconds in the black water, the old man panicked, thrashing his arms and legs. His knee struck me in the face and I lost my grip on his hand.

We rose, gasping in the six inches of air remaining at the rounded ceiling.

"You man." I rubbed my smarting cheek. "You want die? Little girls out there cry. They cry more if I bring out dead teacher. Stay still for goblin and maybe you live. Yes?"

He grimaced, then put his hand in mine. We dove, my red light shining through the murk.

I led him around a ghostly suspension of white fabric—the tattered remains of the sail, I guessed. The old man's hand tensed in mine, but to his credit, he resisted panic.

We ducked beneath a decorative railing and were free of the craft. I kicked toward the dappled light above, dragging the old man with me.

We arose, spluttering in the air. The waiting crowd shouted and whooped, and a dozen arms reached down to help the old man onto the dock, wrapping him in blankets.

I dove back beneath the water and swam toward where Makozi waited. I pulled myself onto the boardwalk, dripping wet, and draped the red cloak over my head and shoulders.

"Come, Kozi. We buy stamp now."

18

FRIENDS OF THE ABC

I learned the hard way what Makozi meant by *closed*. By the time we returned to the market, the vendors were either gone or busy packing up their goods. They ignored Makozi as he tried to get their attention, and we left without so much as an apple.

The rains fell hard that evening, pattering against sails and decks and soaking into the wood beneath our feet. I leaned against a stack of empty crates, wrapping my arms around Makozi as we huddled under the Master's cloak. I heard his stomach rumble, and that made me feel worse than my own gnawing hunger.

Makozi sniffled, tears mingling with the raindrops on his face.

"Hey," I said, drawing his shivering body closer. "Magma learn better song."

"With real words?"

"Real words. You want hear?"

He nodded.

I cleared my throat.

> *There is a boy,*
> *Hims eyes are brown,*
> *Hims hairs are black,*
> *Hims name is Kozi.*

There was a long pause after I finished. Makozi wiped his nose and asked, "Is that all there is?"

"Yes."

"Did you make that up?"

"I did," I confessed.

"Well," he said in a diplomatic tone, "it's really not too good." He pressed his head into my chest and squeezed his arms around me. "Sing it again."

Before I could start over, a figure dropped in front of us, as though he'd fallen from the sky.

"Hey, Hobgoblin." It was a skinny boy, a head taller than us, who wore a dirty tunic of mismatched colors against his nearly obsidian skin. He smiled, revealing a mouthful of crooked teeth.

"Hey, Hobgoblin," he repeated.

Makozi poked me in the side. "He means you, Magma."

The lanky boy cocked his head. "How many people you got under your coat?"

Makozi popped his head out of the opening. "Only me."

"Well, Hobgoblin and Only Me, my name's Gangle. And the lady of the house says you follow me."

I narrowed my eyes. "Follow to where?"

"Follow me to the ABC."

"*Ay-bee-see*? I not know *Ay-bee-see*."

"Asuka's Boat Cuisine!" He slapped his thigh as though telling a joke.

I stared.

Makozi tugged at my tunic. "He means food, Magma."

"Food, and such food," Gangle said.

"Can we go, Magma?"

I sighed. I was far too exhausted and overwhelmed to be suspicious anymore. And I had to get Makozi fed.

I rose to my feet, pulling the child up with me. "We come."

Gangle started down the wet boardwalk, working his way around a pile of broken glass and a man sleeping under a tarp. Makozi and I followed. He led us through the maze of docks, often stopping to do stupid things like whistle at the size of a particularly large ship or kick ceramic shards into the river and laugh at the splash.

Were *all* human children like this?

The boy finally led us to a sturdy boat with a house-like structure on top, covered by a metal roof that pinged in the rain. Gangle leapt over the railing of the boat and rapped his knuckles on a wooden door. Makozi and I boarded as well, our clothes dripping. I swallowed and pulled my hood over my face. I'd never been in a human home before.

The wooden door creaked open. A grubby young woman stood in the lamplight, wearing a threadbare robe tied back with a large tattered bow. Her brownish-black hair fell straight around her sandy beige face.

"Oh, you found them."

"Yep," said Gangle, holding out his hand.

The slender girl placed a ball of white grains into his palm. Gangle bowed and then leapt over the boat's railing. He landed on the boardwalk with a flourish of his hand, then disappeared into the rain.

The girl turned to us. "Come in, out of the wet." I followed, noting that this human was a foot and a half taller than me—not quite an adult, I guessed, but close. Did humans also have an adolescent stage?

She led us to a small interior room, crowded with wooden crates and dangling rectangles of fabric. As I expected, the placed reeked of humanity. But there were other aromas, too: smoke, and a scented steam that rose up from the center of the room, where a small fire burned. A matronly woman stirred a pot, her greying hair tied in a topknot.

The girl behind us urged us forward. "I'm Etsuko, and this is my mother, Asuka."

The woman kneeling by the pot looked up from her stirring, then pointed her wooden spoon at me. "Let me see your face."

I braced myself for what could be a volatile reaction to my goblin features, then drew back my hood.

But Asuka only nodded. "So he *did* find you. Gangle wasn't telling stories this time."

"Did you really pull Old Folorunso from a sinking dhow?" Etsuko asked.

Makozi beamed. "She sure did."

"Who Old Fol—Folo—?" I stammered.

"Old Folorunso," Estuko said. "It *is* a mouthful."

"Hims is great man?"

"Not by the usual ways of measuring it," said Asuka. "But he's greatly respected on the docks. He's one of the few citizens of B'jeme who remembers his friendship with us Centrals."

Makozi furrowed his brow. "Centrals? I thought you were Tsuru."

Etsuko laughed. "We are. But 'Centrals' means anyone who travels here to trade at Vindor's Central Market, regardless of nationality." The girl regarded me, curiosity sparkling in her brown eyes. "We see people from all over Vindor here, but I've never met a goblin. What kind of goods do you trade?"

It took me a moment to untangle her question. She spoke quickly, and her accent was different than Makozi's.

"Oh, I not trade," I answered. "I finded Kozi in woods. He is from *Jem*—"

"*Bjem*," Asuka corrected, adding an impossible consonant in the front.

"Uh, yes. Hims from here, but he got lost. I bringing him back." I nudged the boy. "Say your name."

"I'm Makozi Ibenwo."

I turned back to the women. "You know hims family?"

"Oh, we're not from the city," Etsuko said. "But maybe Mareso would know."

Asuka tilted her head. "You found him in the woods?"

Before I could explain, there was a knock at the door. Etsuko rose and escorted in another woman, wearing a dusty pink robe with large geometric patterns. Her skin was the same deep, earthy black as Makozi's—except for her arms and hands, which were a bright fuchsia.

She knelt and placed a hairy kind of root next to the cooking pot.

"For tomorrow's soup, Asuka-san."

The matron nodded and filled up a clay bowl with fragrant liquid from the pot. The woman took it with her unnaturally pink hands and sat on the rough wooden floorboards. Only then did she seem to notice Makozi and me.

"I see we've added to the ABC. A fellow dye worker, I take it?" Fuchsia Hands pointed to my red-stained fingers.

"Um ..." I definitely didn't want to explain my tattoos.

"She's the one who saved Old Foloronso," Etsuko said.

"Ah, I heard about that." Fuchsia smiled. "You are welcome here."

"Hers know Kozi's family?" I asked Etsuko.

"No. She *is* Dembeyan like those in B'jeme, but she's from N'gozi, a different city. That makes her a Central like us."

Asuka rummaged around her crates and found a child-sized bowl, which she filled with steaming soup.

"Thank you." Makozi took the bowl and used a battered metal utensil to shovel the broth into his mouth.

I held out the Bandit King's mug and Asuka ladled the mysterious liquid inside.

Following Makozi's lead, I used the spoon to poke at the various items in the bowl. I didn't want to appear rude, but I had no idea if I could even eat this food. I tasted each item bit by bit, whispering questions to Makozi.

The white substance that he called *rice* was starchy and bland, but filling. A few different kinds of plant materials floated in the bowl, including an orange tuber that was too sweet to consume. But I was glad to find some mushrooms and a flat green leaf that was refreshingly bitter.

Etsuko offered me a soft green plant called *pickle* that almost killed me, though. My whole face burned from the acidity for several minutes.

Another knock at the door. Two men entered, smelling especially human. They must have really worked up a sweat today. My eyes watered.

These men wore loose, cream-colored shirts and baggy red trousers. Their dark hair was wavy, their bronze skin somewhere in between Etsuko's beige and Makozi's black. One of the men had hair sprouting from his chin, and I tried not to stare.

His smooth-faced companion held out an item wrapped in cloth. "For tomorrow's soup, Asuka-san," he said with a grin.

Asuka pulled back some of the cloth, revealing the largest haunch of meat I'd ever seen.

The matron shook her head. "That is too much, Bahor-san."

"It's salt-cured and smoked," the bare-faced man replied. "Use it to spice up the soup for the next two weeks."

"And then you can boil the bone for broth," said Hair-Face.

"Our uncle sent it to us on the last resupply wagon," said the bare-faced man. "We didn't feel right not sharing it. Consider us paid for a while."

"Hmph," Asuka said, but she let Bare-Face place the meat on the mat beside Fuchsia's root.

Meanwhile I couldn't stop staring at this enormous piece of flesh. "How you get such big meat?" I blurted out.

The two wavy-haired men looked at me.

"Oh, hello," said Hair-Face. "Didn't see you there. It's leg of goat, a Nomad staple."

My mouth dropped open. "That just the *leg*?"

Makozi giggled.

"I don't know *goat*," I confessed.

"Oh, goats, you've got to know goats," said Bare-Face. "Nomad life revolves around goats, almost entirely."

"And horses," added Hair-Face.

"She didn't ask about horses, brother."

"She ought to know about horses, too."

I frowned. "I not know *goat*."

"Ah, then, let the experts explain."

The two brothers then launched into a confusing description of a creature that had four stiff legs, stones for feet, hot blood, yellow devil eyes, and long hair all over its body and especially on its face. Goat had so much hair the Nomad people could adorn themselves in it. Goat could jump over mountains and grew spikes on its head like weapons. If provoked, Goat could scream like a man.

It seemed to me such a monster would put the Blindwyrm to shame.

"But you mans," I said, "you not fierce and you have soft hands. How mans catch such awful beast?"

The humans in the room all burst into laughter. Even Makozi —the child I'd traded my Master's pin for, who I'd dragged to this city at the risk of my own freedom—even Makozi laughed at me.

But then he threw his skinny arms around my neck and nestled into my chest, giggling. "Oh, Magma."

I glanced around the crowded room and noticed something new. This human laughter was not meant to shame or degrade me. If anything, it seemed to make them softer toward me.

Humans stank to high heaven, but I was starting to like them.

"Now I have a question for you, little goblin," said Hair-Face. "What kind of a name is *Magma?*"

"I don't know what kind of name is Magma. Kozi thought it."

Makozi nodded. "Thought it up inside my own head."

"Do you know what the word means?" Fuchsia asked.

I narrowed my eyes. What kind of weird name had this child saddled me with?

"Magma is a kind of stone from deep under the earth," the pink-handed woman continued. "It gets so warm that it melts and glows with a bright light."

"Ah, I know it," I said.

The dinner party at the ABC settled into a comfortable quiet, the only sounds the clink of utensils against bowls and rain against the metal roof.

Wait a minute. My given name was *Valshara*, or obsidian—melted stone that hardened into razor-sharp glass. This boy had somehow given me a name the was the exact reversal of that—stone that softened until it gave warmth and light.

Something about that name felt right. I hugged Makozi a little closer.

19

THE MISERY POLICIES

A knock came at the boat's wooden door. "Am I too late?"
Etsuko rose quickly, tripping over her own feet. "Oh,
Mareso! Please, come in."

A young Dembeyan man entered. His robe was a bright goldenrod, emblazoned with large red triangles and squares, the fabric
noticeably bright and crisp against his rich black skin. He sat
down on the floor, and placed a large sack of vegetables beside the
other gifts. "For tomorrow's soup, Asuka-san."

The matronly woman smiled. "It's almost gone. Eat up,
quickly."

Etsuko's eyes followed the young Dembeyan as he sat down
with his bowl, but he didn't look her way again.

Etsuko tapped me on the shoulder. "Mareso is the one you
should ask."

"Ask me what?" Mareso asked.

I roused Makozi, who had started to doze beside me. "I'm
Makozi Ibenwo," he said sleepily.

"You know hims family?"

The young man stroked his chin. He had just a small shadow
of black hair on his face, close against his skin, and the hair on his
scalp was not much longer. I wondered why this man's hair came

in so short while Makozi had been born with hair so long and tangled.

"Can't say I recognize the family name Makozi," he said.

"Ibenwo," I corrected. "Hims family Ibenwo."

Mareso laughed. "I'm afraid you have that backwards, my little green friend. We Dembeyans put the family name before the personal one. This child is named Ibenwo."

I shot Makozi a look. Had he really let me call him the wrong name *this whole time*? "Kozi, why you not say so?"

He yawned and leaned into my shoulder. "I like when you call me Kozi."

I sighed and turned back to Mareso. "You know the family Makozi then?"

"No one immediately comes to mind," Mareso said. "But there are hundreds of families in B'jeme. It's a city of nearly eight thousand people."

My mouth opened. *How* many people lived behind those walls?

"Is he a citizen?" Mareso asked.

"He say hims from B'jeme. I finded him in the woods and bringed him back here."

"What was he doing in the woods?"

I paused for a moment, waiting for Makozi's breathing to become deep and regular. When I was certain he was asleep, I spoke quietly.

"I finded him in Wood Shed. Hims not with mama. The shining mans have him in ring, hold him with strong magic. I got in and buyed him and bring him back here."

The small group of humans stared at me. Even the Nomad brothers were quiet for a moment.

"You—you entered a fairy ring?" Etsuko asked, breathless. "How? You can't pass through the charmed border unless you know something's there."

I shrugged. "I want to see why air have burning magic smell."

Hair-Face laughed. "You can *smell* magic?" He elbowed his

brother. "Oh, that's too good. It would take a hundred men a hundred years to locate a fairy court, and she just sniffs it out on one try."

His comment didn't sit well with me. Was that the reason Makozi's mother didn't come back for him—because she couldn't find him?

Asuka stacked up her guests' empty bowls. "Magma-san," she said with a careful tone, "did you see his mother?"

"I not finded her." I left out the reasons I'd needed to move on before doing a thorough search of the woods. I wondered now if I'd made a bigger mistake than I'd thought. "I hope she in B'jeme, waiting for Makozi."

Asuka opened her mouth as though to say something, then pursed her lips closed.

"But," I said at length. "We not have stamp to get into gate. Not me, not Makozi." I looked around at the assembled diners. "You know mans who sell stamps?"

"Ha," Etsuko said. "Do you have a small fortune?"

"*Fortune*? I don't know *fortune*."

"She means it's very, very expensive to buy a stamp," Mareso said.

I considered for moment, then reached into my pocket and pulled out a single amethyst crystal. I placed it in Mareso's hand.

"Is this *fortune*?"

Mareso looked at the jewel, his dark eyes wide. "This is quite the gemstone," he said, handing it back. "It would buy many goods in the market. But sadly you'd need about twenty of these to buy stamps for you and the boy."

My eyes widened. "So many? How any man buy stamp?"

"We can't," Etsuko said bitterly.

Mareso looked at my boy's sleeping form. "If he's from the city, he should have a stamp. They do have to be re-applied after a couple of months or they fade away. How long was he in Woodshea?"

I hadn't actually thought about that. When I rescued him

from the pixies, Makozi acted as though he'd seen his mother only minutes before. But the fairies' spell did seem to have altered his memories. How long *had* he been abducted for?

"Check his forearm when you get a chance," Mareso said, nodding toward Makozi's figure curled up beside me. "You'll be looking for something like this."

Mareso pulled up his yellow sleeve, revealing a large, black square painted onto the dark skin near his wrist. A series of squiggles and symbols crowded inside the square outline.

"If there's even a trace of a stamp, the guards may let him in."

I knew for a fact I hadn't seen anything like that on Makozi.

"How you get stamp?" I asked.

Mareso shrugged. "Citizen of B'jeme, born and bred. I just choose to spend time here with my Central friends."

"Men like Mareso have grown rare," Asuka said.

I pondered this for a minute. "So. One type of mans is Citizen, live in B'jeme. All have stamps. They go through gate. Other type of mans are Centrals, not have stamps, not can go through gate. Must pay *fortune*. This is because Citizen and Central not friends?"

"Not often now. But we used to be," the hairy-faced Nomad said. "Once it was easy to find lodging in a friendly citizen's home. We were welcomed and fed in exchange for conversation and stories."

"Hospitality to strangers is a key virtue in traditional B'jeme culture," Mareso explained. "As the old city motto goes, 'Strength through wisdom and generosity.'"

Something about that sounded familiar.

"Vindor's Central Market has been outside B'jeme's walls as long as anyone can remember," Mareso said. "Once we valued the people and fresh ideas the market brought to us, not just the physical things. We were happy to open our city."

"But now gate *closed*," I said. "Stamps cost *fortune*."

"The gates open if you pay," Etsuko said. "Olayo is still convinced we have the gold and are just being stubborn."

"Who?"

"Olayo." Mareso sighed. "He was elected Mayor two years ago after promising a new era of prosperity for B'jeme. Once in power, Olayo turned on our friends at the Central Market. He imagines a river of gold flowing just outside our walls, and is determined to redirect it through our gates."

"It started with the Hospitality Laws," Bare-Face said, "forbidding citizens to host Centrals."

"No, it started earlier than that," said Mareso. "Olayo campaigned with stories of boorish Central thieves who made off with family heirlooms in the night. He convinced the kind-hearted people of B'jeme that if they hadn't been robbed yet, it was only a matter of time. Hosts closed their doors long before the law required them to do so."

I was familiar with this kind of tactic. The Masters often pitted neutral goblin clans against one another. In-fighting drew attention away from the oppressive Masters, and it ensured the populace was too divided to mount any meaningful resistance.

Fuchsia crossed her pink arms. "By banishing us from citizen homes, Olayo figures we'll happily pay for his new inns within the city. But then he increased the price of stamps a thousand-fold. We can't afford to get to his meager beds."

"Most of us decided just to sleep on the docks," Hair-Face said. "Olayo didn't like that. Now he tries to strong-arm us into paying by making dock life as difficult as possible."

"The 'Misery Policies,'" Bare-Face said.

"*Misery* how?" I asked.

"Well, take the new Vendor License," Fuchsia said. "You're no longer able to just set up shop for a few days. Each merchant has to pay an exorbitant fee each time they arrive at the market."

"It means most of us can't afford to go back home," Etsuko said. "Mother and I only intended to sell our silks for a week. We've been trapped here for five months, waiting for our village to send us enough silk so we can escape our debt."

"And while we wait, we go hungry," said Bare-Face. "Our

wagons can't hold months' worth of food and still have room for wool."

"When some of us citizens noticed our Central friends going without meals, we brought it up to the Mayor," Mareso said. "His response? New taxes on food sales outside the city walls. It's made hunger worse."

"Not to mention the tax on clean water," Hair-Face added.

"Olayo thinks if he can just squeeze us hard enough, we'll bleed money into his coffers," Fuchsia said. "And he's convinced B'jeme's citizens that we're ragged and sick and thin because we're bad people."

I looked at the rag-tag humans before me, taking note of the leanness of their faces and their faded clothing. "If Mayor make you so misery, why not you go home?"

Hair-Face shrugged. "We have to sell wool so we can buy salt from the Mauritians. Our tribe can't preserve food without it."

"Our village's entire economy depends on us selling silks to other nations," Etsuko said. "This is the largest market in Vindor."

The room fell into a thoughtful silence.

I wasn't here to get entangled in human politics. My job was to get Makozi back home, then get back to running for my life. But I did feel sorry for this group of people—especially since they'd so kindly shared their precious food with me.

Human society was more complex than I'd anticipated. To be honest, I'd just assumed humans were knuckle-dragging barbarians who scratched homes in the dirt because they didn't have the sense to go underground.

The sound of rain on the roof grew quieter, and the friends of ABC took advantage of the lull to get back to their own abodes— whatever pitiful kinds of shelters those may had been. Asuka's boat seemed to be one of the few with a watertight roof.

At last it was only us and Asuka left. I rolled up my Master's cloak and guided Makozi's head off of my lap and onto its soft fabric. He snored a bit without waking up.

I approached Asuka and bowed at the waist, the way I'd seen the other guests do.

"For tomorrow's soup, Asuka-san," I said, pressing an amethyst into her palm.

"No," the matron said sharply. "Do you wish to insult me? You are a guest, and this is too fine a price for mere soup."

"What about bed?" I glanced over at Makozi. "Can *fortune* buy dry bed for Kozi until we get to city?"

Asuka put the jewel back into my hand. "He may sleep here, but as a guest. I insist."

I bowed my head, gratitude overwhelming me. "Thanks you. I ... I not know how to care for boy. I not know how hims eat or what hims need."

"By the looks of it, you're doing a fine job."

I swallowed back a lump in my throat. "He needs hims mama."

I placed the Bandit King's mug by Makozi's head, so if he awoke in the night he'd know I'd be back soon. Then I moved toward the door.

"Magma-san, won't you spend the night here too?"

I shook my head. "Thanks you, but boat is too warm for goblin to sleep." That was true. I also needed a respite from the odors, but I didn't mention that.

Most importantly, I had to study the walls of B'jeme. If I was going to get Makozi home, I'd have to break my way in.

20

TAJIM'S WHEEL

The earthen wall of B'jeme stood before me, its imposing height gleaming in the distant torchlight. I pressed my hand against its slick surface, a thin coating of mud clinging to my palm.

If the wall had seemed daunting to climb while dry, it was going to be impossible when wet.

I'd come to the corner of the city, a stone's throw from the last of the market tents and uncomfortably close to the enormous wheel contraption. On one side of the boardwalk, the wooden spokes creaked and splashed as they dipped into the river water. On the wall side, six heavy rods rose and fell tirelessly in their iron cylinders.

Unlike the market, it seemed the wheel was never *closed*.

Whatever this crazy human invention was, climbing on top of it was not an option, not with all those moving parts.

Perhaps there was a tree along the forest side of the city that I could scale—or better yet, maybe I could hoist Makozi over the wall, if I found a suitable branch and a rope long enough.

A voice drifted from somewhere behind me. I startled—I'd thought the Market would be empty at this hour. Would a guard watching me study the wall guess what I was planning?

The voice continued—breathy and tremulous—followed by the soft click of wooden sandals on the dock. I glanced up and saw a thin girl with straight hair, the bedraggled bow at her back soaked with rain. She was singing.

"Etsuko?"

"Magma, what are you doing here?"

I straightened. "I not do a thing. What Etsuko do here?"

"Nothing. I just like to walk in the rain." Etsuko glanced out at the river, her eyes wistful, then turned back to me. "Have you not found a place to sleep yet? If you need to stay with us, please do."

"No, I ..." I cast around for an excuse. "This noisy wheel, too loud for sleep."

"Oh. I suppose most of us Centrals have just gotten used to the sound."

"What it do?"

Etsuko scratched her elbow. "Mareso explained it to me once. When it rains too hard in the city, the streets flood. So years ago the citizens dug a drain system beneath the roads to channel the rainwater to the river.

"But later the river shifted closer to the city walls. Water can now flow up into the drain tunnels, flooding the streets from beneath. So a clever citizen named Tajim built this. The river current turns the wheel, and the wheel makes the pistons move up and down. Somehow that movement pulls water out of the drains and keeps the streets dry."

I recalled the gurgling sound I'd heard inside the cylinders. "Ah, yes. Thanks you," I said. "I go find quiet sleep place now."

I made a show of heading back toward the docks.

"I hope ..." Etsuko hesitated. "I hope Makozi *does* have a stamp. I'd hate for him to end up like Gangle."

I remembered crooked-toothed boy from the docks. "What happen Gangle?"

"He was fleeing a bad home situation in another Dembeyan city—K'wambe, maybe?—and came here looking for an uncle or something. But he arrived just as Mayor Olayo established the stamp laws. Of course Gangle doesn't have that kind of money. We Centrals take care of him the best we can, but ..." Her voice trailed off.

"Ah."

That cemented my plan. I had to smuggle Makozi into the city any way possible, find his family, and get out before the guards caught wind of my presence.

A wave of emotion hit me—not just because of the sheer improbability of this task, but because I'd be leaving Makozi behind in a city I'd never be able to re-enter. I swallowed hard.

"Have a good night, Magma," Etsuko said. "Let us know if you need anything." She resumed her stroll, a faint song on her lips.

A few minutes later the rain poured harder than ever, and I huddled inside an overturned barrel for shelter. Water pounded on the wood above me and I shivered, squeezing my eyes shut.

When I opened them, I was inside the city. The walls stretched into the night sky, looming over me on every side. And down a muddy street I saw the woman in red.

I scrambled after her, tripping over boats and wheels and other objects that didn't make sense on a city walkway. The woman had the same deep black skin as Makozi's, and her long red dress was in the B'jeme style. There was something else familiar about the pattern of the cloth, but I didn't have time to figure it out—as before, the woman remained forever in the distance, no matter how hard I ran.

She came to the mouth of a tunnel that opened right into the city square. The woman glanced back at me with dark and mournful eyes, then disappeared into the darkness.

I woke from my dream with a start. *Tunnels.*

The city of B'jeme had an entire system of tunnels beneath its streets. Surely some of the storm drains would be large enough for Makozi and me to squeeze through.

I crept out of my barrel shelter to find the rain had long

stopped, a greyish light playing on the horizon. I hurried toward Tajim's Wheel, hoping the guards hadn't started their rounds yet.

I stopped in front of the massive contraption, watching the restless motion of the spokes and pistons. If this thing was pumping water out of the tunnels, surely there had to be an entrance nearby.

Keeping a safe distance away from the moving wheel, I slid over to the edge of the boardwalk, peering into the dark river below. *Well, here goes.*

For a moment, my body dangled from the edge of the wooden planks. Then I dropped into the cold current, swimming beneath the pier and toward the city wall. Its surface was slick with mud, but here at the foundation stood huge blocks of stone.

Drawing a deep breath, I submerged myself beneath the water, feeling my way around the wall. I found the drain entrance within a minute of searching—an even circle in a hard clay, opening into a tunnel about three feet in diameter. Quite spacious compared to what I was used to.

I popped back up to the river surface to take a breath, then dove and kicked my way into the clay pipe, using the red lights on my fingertips to guide me. The water churned in my ears, along with a gurgling sound.

The pipe angled upward, and I followed where it led. The gurgle grew more intense, and for a moment, the water seemed to pull backward.

I had one hand on the ceiling of the pipe, feeling my way, and suddenly I felt the cool sensation of dry air. I tilted my head back and managed to get my nose and mouth above the surface, taking in the precious oxygen.

I paddled a little further up the angled tunnel and found the water level lower with every stroke.

At last I crouched in the dark tunnel, my cloak and linen clothes dripping. Somewhere beyond the pipe's clay wall, water swooshed away, pulsing with the regular squeaks and groans of Tajim's mechanism.

The humans deserved credit: their contraption worked brilliantly. Small rivulets of rainwater flowed past my feet—the last vestiges of the night's rainfall—but the clay at the top of the tunnel was dry and seemed to have been for quite some time.

I crawled through the dark pipe, moving deeper into the city and feeling strangely at ease. There was something about being in an enclosed space that was like drawing a blanket around my shoulders. The air was still and cool and reliable again. For the first time since I'd left the caverns, I felt at home.

The unnatural Topside world with its open spaces and unpredictable weather had been eating at me more than I'd realized. This tunnel system had to be the only place in miles suitable for goblin biology. But I didn't have time to get comfortable—I needed to chart a path into the city above, and then get out before the guards discovered what I was doing.

A shaft of grey light illuminated the tunnel ahead of me. I craned my neck to see a small vertical opening that rose five feet or so, topped in a clay grate that was silhouetted against the faint sunlight.

That had to be the street level. Rainwater dripped from the grate above and splashed into the pipe where I crouched. Was this narrow shaft the only link to the street, though? I could barely fit my arm through there.

I continued on, hoping to find a more substantial street entrance. The pipe kept angling upwards, and now and then I'd see a dark corridor where another clay pipe fed into this one.

I'd hate to be down here during a flood.

I could still hear the whooshing of water through unseen channels and the metallic creaks of Tajim's Wheel. The squeaks and groans that had at first seemed random were actually quite regular, the rhythm of it seeping into my bones.

The tunnel I crawled through opened up into a large chamber. Multiple passages fed into the round room from all directions, with no obvious path forward.

I stood, stretching my legs and trying to decide which tunnel to take. These tunnels were human-made, and thus there should be logic to them. It was a puzzle that I might be able to crack if I just thought it through.

I studied each pipe entrance for some sort of clue. The mechanical groans continued in the background. A new sound element had been added in this chamber, though—a kind of rumbling, almost wheezing sound.

Oddly, it didn't fit the familiar pattern. Sometimes the wheeze was completely out of sync, and then a few seconds later it matched up again. Strange.

At the top of the chamber I found the entrance to one of those vertical shafts. This one was wide enough for me to fit through, if I could just reach it. I shone my red light at the rim and was surprised to find a thick loop of wire protruding from the wall. A handle? Ah—there was another one above it, and one above that. A ladder.

Perhaps this was a maintenance chamber, in which men could come up and down to do repairs. A patch of sunlight shone through a grate above.

I'd found the way up. The first metal rung was some distance above me, but I might be able to grasp it if I jumped.

I was just tensing my legs to prepare for the leap when the back of my neck prickled. The wheezing sound was louder than ever.

Something here wasn't right.

That wheezing—could it be breathing? Was there a guard watching me?

No, a human couldn't breathe that loudly. At that volume, it would have to be coming from a remarkably large creature, huge but narrow enough to fit in a pipe ...

The horrible realization clicked into place too late.

I spun to face the tunnel behind me and caught sight of the flickering tongue. The six-horned head pushed its way into the chamber's grey light, then rose up above me on its serpentine body. The Blindwyrm.

21

WHAT LURKS BENEATH

The Blindwyrm's mouth opened, exposing its curved fangs. I stood, half-mesmerized. My entire body could easily fit into that gaping purple maw.

Then all was a blur as the monster lunged toward me.

I dodged into the nearest tunnel just as it struck. Its fang grazed the back of my calf and I hissed in pain.

If Blindwyrms were venomous, I'd know soon enough. But I wasn't waiting around.

I scrambled down the tunnel I'd chosen at random. The even clay surface offered no obstacles to slow down the Blindwyrm on my heels. Still, I was able to get a decent head start—the straightness of the pipes seemed to make its undulating movement difficult.

Galloping down the tunnel on all fours, I cursed my idiocy. These tunnels were the only place suitable for a goblin, so where else would the Faceless wait to ambush me?

The Faceless—was he down one of these other paths, his blow dart at the ready? Not that there was anything I could do to avoid him.

My feet splashed in water. Mercifully, I'd chosen a pipe that opened up into the river. I inhaled and dove into the submerged tunnel. A moment later, I felt the water surge as the Blindwyrm splashed in behind me.

I beat against the water in total darkness, too afraid to use my red light. The Blindwyrm wouldn't be able to detect it, but the Faceless, wherever he was, might.

The water grew brighter. I'd made it out of the pipe and into the sunlit river.

I surfaced and grabbed onto one of the pier's support poles, digging my claws into the wood and hoisting myself onto the dock. I squinted in the morning light.

Humans milling around the market glanced up at my dripping form, only mildly interested.

Then a woman screamed.

The Blindwyrm's wickedly horned head bubbled up from the river. The monster drew itself up like a cobra, towering above the docks and preparing to strike again. People pushed each other toward the market, desperate to get away.

I couldn't stay on the dock, couldn't run toward the market and put the vendors in danger. I glanced into the water and spied a derelict rowboat, its anchor rope trailing uselessly beside it.

I threw myself into it with a thud, just as the Blindwyrm's fangs glanced against the dock plank I'd just been standing on.

Great, a boat. Where were the steering stick things? As always, my impulse had led me astray.

The eyeless head turned toward me—no fooling the Blindwyrm's senses. I drew back and tripped over something on the floor of the boat.

The oar. I dunked it into the water and pushed with all my might. The rowboat spun around in a circle. Stupid.

I jumped overboard, swimming furiously as the Blindwyrm's fangs sank deep into the wood. The whole boat went under, then bobbed back up as the Blindwyrm tried to shake it out of its mouth. The rowboat was lodged in its teeth.

Paddling myself toward the center of the river, I fought the current and nearly got plowed over by a merchant's dhow.

Glancing back, I saw the Blindwyrm had freed itself of the boat. It undulated through the water, hot on my trail. The black tongue flickered mere yards from my toes.

It opened its mouth wide and I could feel the heat of its breath with an odor like rotten flesh.

I flailed my arms and legs, my swimming becoming sloppy in my panic. My body locked up, and I anticipated the dagger-like fangs hitting their mark this time. The Blindwyrm raised its head behind me.

Then it stopped, its tongue flickering wildly. With a jerk of its neck, the Blindwyrm veered away from me, speeding back toward the docks.

I tread water for a moment, dumbfounded. What could the Blindwyrm have sensed that would cause it to abandon its—?

The water around me bubbled and churned. The river current reversed, and I found myself pushed backward by a wave —a pulse of water that originated from somewhere beneath me.

A huge white curve of bone broke through the surface of the water, rising up to my left. I spluttered and turned around, only to see an identical curve to my right. The two upside-down arcs of ivory continued to rise into the sky.

Then, behind the retreating form of the Blindwyrm, an enormous white serpent emerged from the water, almost as thick as the black dragon it pursued.

But the head wasn't right. It wasn't a head at all. It had gaping black holes instead of eyes, and the whole thing opened and closed like a set of lips. The entire organism was as flexible and boneless as an earthworm.

Screams from the docks snapped me out of my stupor. I struggled against the current, trying to get away from whatever this new monstrosity was.

I swam around the curved bone that was now ten feet in the air and still rising. I didn't want to find out what kind of creature could have tusks this long.

The serpentine tentacle wrapped the Blindwyrm in its lip-like ends, as easily as I might pick up a stick. The black serpent panicked, writhing and biting to no avail.

The water roiled again. Something larger still bubbled up from beneath the river's surface. Its wake slammed me into the stern of a stocky merchant ship. I managed to grasp onto the vessel's railing, while terrified sailors on board wrestled their craft toward the docks.

A smooth white dome arose from the water, with huge white sails on either side. I realized with a start that these were ears, connected to a head nine feet wide, continuing to rise. A second later I could see the monstrous eye—a round globe with a pinkish hue to it.

And then it became clear—everything was part of the same creature. The serpent-like tentacle connected to this terrible face, between the curved tusks and above the enormous mouth.

The tentacle raised the Blindwyrm into the morning sky for a second, then flipped downward and stuffed it into the creature's maw. It crunched down, breaking the Blindwyrm's back in one bite.

The black serpent went limp and dropped into the water, disappearing without even a bubble trail.

I leapt from the merchant ship and landed on the end of a pier. Sailors from various nations rushed past me. Abandoned boats bashed against the docks in the churning water.

A huge white hill appeared behind the tusked head—the creature's back, large as an island. The monster was half-submerged in the river—if it had legs, I couldn't see them—but it seemed to finally have come to rest.

The only movement now was a figure in blue that walked along the white ridge of the creature's back.

A human woman.

Silence fell over the docks as the woman stepped onto the monster's head. It blinked serenely beneath her feet.

"Well, well." The woman's skin was a deep brown, and

hundreds of tiny braids fell all the way to her waist. She carried a silver scepter with a huge lapis lazuli at the end.

"Olayo, you scoundrel." The woman's alto voice carried over the river easily. "So this is where you've been hiding. *Tsk.* Olayo, don't tell me you've forgotten our agreement. Well, they say an elephant never forgets, and neither does Zaraiyah."

At that moment, a large gold-trimmed ship approached the port. The centaurs on the deck saw the monstrous island too late, and they shouted as they tried to turn the ship away. But the size of the vessel and the river current worked against them.

The woman Zaraiyah glared at them, then made a small movement with her silver scepter as though swatting at a fly.

The monster beneath her swung its serpentine trunk, smashing into the ship and flipping it over. Centaur sailors splashed into the water, struggling in the wreckage of their vessel.

Zaraiyah continued over the sailors' cries as though nothing had happened. "You have forty-eight hours to return to me what you owe, Olayo, or we will trample your city and drag you out screaming." She turned and retreated down the monster's back. "We'll be waiting."

22

OLD FOLORUNSO

The docks were chaos as I fought my way back to Makozi.

Merchants tore down their tents and grabbed armloads of whatever goods they had—gold jewelry, piles of scrolls, sacks of vegetables, bolts of colored fabric—and stuffed them into dhows, rowboats, and rafts.

But as the watercraft left the docks, the monster swiped at them with its flexible trunk. It overturned several before the crowd abandoned the idea of water travel. Some hunkered down in their docked boats, while others fled toward the woods.

City guards shouted instructions at the throngs of people, trying in vain to impose order.

I struggled through the confusion, praying that Asuka's houseboat hadn't been one of the capsized vessels.

Thankfully, I found it docked in its familiar spot. I ran to the door and heard voices within.

"I don't care about losses," Asuka was saying. "Debt is nothing compared to seeing my only child crushed by a *kaiju*."

"Mother, we can't. Who will feed the ABC if we leave?"

Asuka paused. "Just don't leave the boat, Etsuko. I don't want you anywhere near danger."

"Mother, I—"

Asuka cleared her throat as I entered. Etsuko stopped her protest and scooped me up in an embrace. "Oh, Magma, isn't it terrible?"

"Where Kozi?"

Asuka motioned to the corner, where my boy slept despite the cacophony around him. I exhaled.

The less he knew, the better. We were leaving B'jeme, now.

A sharp rap at the door. Asuka and Etsuko glanced at each other, and Etsuko opened it.

A guard in olive green stood in the doorway, with Gangle at his side. The crooked-toothed boy pointed at me. "There she is."

I froze. They'd found out about my sneaking through the drains, and they were coming to—

The guard turned to someone behind him I couldn't see. "Are you sure this is necessary, sir? The timing really isn't ideal."

"Let me see her," said a cheerful voice.

The guard stepped back, and an old man in a long grey tunic stepped into the doorway, his short white curls tight against his scalp. He looked familiar somehow, though I couldn't place him.

"Folorunso?" Asuka asked. "What are you doing out here? Go back to the safety of the city."

"Nonsense," the old man said. "I want to see the goblin who saved my life."

The man from the sinking dhow. Of course. I stepped forward.

He kneeled and grasped my hand with both of his, his large palms warm against my skin. "I never got a chance to thank you for saving my life. You put yourself in harm's way to save an old man you didn't know. Thank you, from the bottom of my heart."

I smiled weakly, finding his exuberance awkward.

"I want to repay you in some way," he continued. "Name anything you want, anything. Old Folorunso has many friends and I can make things happen."

I blinked for a moment, trying to make sure I was correctly understanding him. "Stamp," I blurted.

His forehead wrinkled. "What?"

"I need stamp, for me and boy." I pointed at the sleeping Makozi. "Hims lost and hims family inside B'jeme. I need to get in to find hims family, then I get out."

"Hmm," Old Folorunso said. "I can't afford two stamps."

My heart fell.

"But that's probably not what you need. I might be able to get you a temporary visa that will let you stay for three days."

"I take it." Three days would be plenty of time to find Makozi's family. He knew his address, after all.

The old man smiled. "I'll escort you to the stamp station."

I nodded my thanks and turned to Makozi. Could this really be so simple? Was this yet another miracle of my new life?

"Kozi, wake. We get stamps. We go home now."

He sat up, running his hands through his matted locks. "Yay," he said with a yawn.

I re-attached the Bandit King's mug to my belt and I hurried Makozi toward the door.

Etsuko stepped in front of me. "Before you go." She held up a long garment of black silk. "I thought you could wear this. I know you don't like the sunlight, and this part here is a veil that goes over your face. Our Rikean customers also live underground, and they find this style protects their sensitive eyes."

She slipped a long black dress over my linen clothes, long enough to hide my green feet, and then adjusted a veil over my face. The headache-inducing brightness of daylight immediately grew bearable.

"You look like a black ghost, Magma." Makozi giggled.

I draped the Master's cloak over my shoulders and raised the hood to conceal the back of my green head and pointed ears. Hiding my goblin features could prove advantageous as I dealt with humans inside the city—humans who might be less open to other species than the Centrals.

"Thanks you, Etsuko." I reached into my pocket and held an amethyst out to her.

"No, Magma." She curled my fingers back over the stone and smiled. "This is a gift. We are friends."

I swallowed back a sudden lump in my throat. In my entire adult life—from the military academy to the Blood Hand force to the Pit—I'd never had an actual friend.

Wouldn't it figure that I would probably never see her again. The minute I got Makozi home, it was back to fleeing the Faceless.

We stepped out of Asuka's doorway onto the sunlit dock, and I recoiled only slightly beneath the dark veil.

"Hey." Makozi pointed toward the river, where the island-sized monster peered at the city with its pink eyes. "Who put our relevant in the water?"

"The what?"

"Relevant. The statue."

I recalled the plaster tree he'd fussed over in the forest, but couldn't see how it was related to this monstrosity. But I had no desire to explain that this was a living creature that meant people harm.

"Oh yes, the relevant," I fudged. "No worry, Kozi. Thems just washing him."

"Good. He did get all dirty. I hope they put them back in the city corner."

We followed Old Folorunso down the docks. He folded his hands behind his back, whistling a tune.

I looked up at him. "You no afraid?"

"Of what?"

I motioned in the direction of the river. "Of the relevant."

"Relevant? More like *ir*relevant." Folorunso chuckled.

I stared at him, and he cleared his throat.

"It's pronounced *elephant*, my little goblin friend. And it's not something to worry about. I've been around a long time, and I know politics when I see it."

"*Politics*? I not know *politics*."

"People in power showing off, and quarreling in the most flamboyant way possible."

"Oh." I scowled, remembering the drama of the Dominion. "I know it."

"It's all just posturing," he said as we wove around clusters of panicking Centrals. "This Zaraiyah woman is some political rival of Olayo's, just making a show of force. The Mayor will come out and meet with her, and they'll figure it out with a secret deal. Each side will tell a story that makes themselves out as the hero. Nothing is getting trampled."

He seemed so sure. But he hadn't been in one of the boats that the monster—the *elephant*—had capsized.

"Listen—do you hear the outgoing drum messages?" The old man waved his hand, and I listened to the incessant knocking patterns in the air. "Not one of them mentions the beast. If the city elders aren't worried, then neither am I."

Only because they're safe inside the city walls. But I was glad to be getting Makozi inside for that very reason.

We passed through the Market. A few vendors remained, trying to hawk wares, but most other booths were abandoned or actively being dismantled by frantic merchants.

I froze in my tracks.

In one of the market tents stood the Faceless. He wore a red Master's cloak, but beneath the hood his face was completely black and featureless.

If that wasn't enough to freeze my blood, out of nowhere a boy appeared beside him.

I gasped. "Makozi!" The Faceless had my child.

A familiar hand squeezed my arm. "What, Magma?"

I turned to Makozi—right beside me, safe. Bewildered, I pointed at his twin beside the Faceless.

He laughed. "Magma, that's us."

"What?"

"It's a mirror. See the frame? Those are reflections. Look." He waved his arms and the other Makozi did the same.

I reached up to touch my hood and the Faceless aped the movement.

I breathed a sigh of relief, most of my fear dissipating. As soon as I stepped away the reflection vanished, the *mirror* now reflecting other vendor tents. This Topside world was exhausting to understand.

My muscles were still tense, however. The Faceless was lurking somewhere in the city right now. In the drains? Hidden in a shadow? Following us through the crowd?

And now I knew a fate worse than him capturing me: him getting hold of Makozi. If he figured out how much the child meant to me, the Faceless would have no qualms about harming him if he found it practical.

I shuddered.

No more letting my emotions get in the way. Makozi wasn't safe until I got him home, far away from me.

The old man led us toward B'jeme's huge keyhole-shaped gate. But instead of climbing the stairs, he turned to a green tent pitched in the shade of the staircase.

A throng of Centrals had gathered outside, some of them clutching gold or fine cloth as they pressed toward the fabric entrance. I realized they were here to buy stamps, sacrificing their treasures for the safety of the city walls.

Olayo was already profiting from this political posturing.

A green-clad guard stood at the entrance. "One at a time. Order, please!" he shouted at the crowd, to no avail.

The sun rose over the eastern tree line as we waited. Finally the guard in charge approached us.

Old Folorunso grinned. "Why, Chelu—you've grown well."

The guard straightened. "Teacher Folorunso, what brings you here, sir?"

"Personal business, Chelu. This one saved my life, and I need to get her and the boy temporary stamps."

"Of course, sir, right this way." The guard drew the fabric door open.

"Thank you, son," the old man said. Makozi and I followed him into the greenish shade of the tent.

"Is he really your son?" Makozi asked.

"Almost." The old man's eye twinkled. "He was my student."

The interior of the stamp tent had a long table and a few chairs, with multiple people moving about.

Makozi drew close to my side, squeezing my hand. "Will it hurt, Magma?"

I glanced at the pile of implements on the table. No knives, no needles, and no piles of glowing coals. "I not think so, Kozi."

The B'jeme system seemed far kinder than any marking system in the Dominion.

"All right," Folorunso said, leading a young man in olive toward us. "My boy Jamal here will take care of you. Who will go first?"

"Me." I held out my arm and the young man rolled up my black sleeve, exposing my inner forearm. In one hand, he held a wooden block with complex carvings on the bottom. He pressed this into a bowl of reddish-brown paste, then pressed it against my wrist.

When he pulled the block off, it left a brown circle a few inches wide and crowded with symbols. The young man then took a small brush and filled in an empty spot. "This pass expires in three days. Don't touch it for another thirty minutes, or you'll smudge the information."

"Did it hurt, Magma?"

I squeezed his hand. "It maybe tickle, Kozi. No fear."

A few minutes later we were climbing the stairs to the gate of B'jeme, following Folorunso. The guards glared at me suspiciously, but when Makozi and I revealed the stamped circles on our forearms, they waved us through without a second thought.

And like a miracle, we entered into the city of B'jeme.

23

THE HOUSE OF MERCY

We stepped through the huge keyhole gate and onto a busy street of worn red cobblestone. Humans—all dark-skinned and colorfully dressed—bustled about, chatting and calling to one another. These citizens were clearly unfazed by the monster watching their city from the river. I myself felt more at ease once behind that enormous wall.

The streets were narrow, hedged in on either side with square buildings of red mud. Vividly painted doors opened into the road, and tapestries of geometric patterns hung along the walls.

The midmorning sun blazed in a cloudless sky, turning the red walls to an intense shade of orange. I was more thankful than ever for Etsuko's veil.

Makozi and I followed Old Folorunso down the first street and through a smaller keyhole opening in a wall.

I stopped. We had come to an intersection of six roads, build-ings squeezed in between them. Each of those streets seemed to lead to another network of roads beyond it. Navigating through this place would be more difficult than I thought.

"Sir," I said, using the term of address his students had given him, "Where Soldier Street?"

The old man waved his hand. "Don't worry about that now. First we've got to get you breakfast."

"Sir, I needs to get Kozi to hims home."

"What's the hurry? You've got three days, after all."

But I've also got a bounty hunter tracking me.

"You can't search on an empty stomach," Old Folorunso said. "The teachers will be happy to share our breakfast with you."

"But—"

"No buts. I insist."

"I want breakfast, Magma," Kozi said. "Please?"

There seemed to be no dissuading the old man from showing us B'jeme's famous hospitality. I sighed and let him lead us deeper through the maze of the city. I tried to keep track of the turns we were making, but every street had the same style of square buildings, impossible to tell apart.

"Look, Magma, the tower."

I followed Makozi's gesture and saw a huge, narrow rectangle reaching high into the blue sky. It was taller than the rest of the city's buildings by double or triple, higher even than the city wall.

"That's where Mayor Olayo lives," Folorunso said.

I squinted up at the building and noticed a wrap-around balcony at the very top. The mayor would be able to see the entire city from here, including the docks beyond the wall.

Did Olayo stand on that balcony and gleefully watch the misery his greed for gold caused?

Actually, if I knew anything about corrupt leaders, the answer was no. He'd be oblivious to the consequences of his choices, more interested in the details of his next banquet or practicing insults for his rivals.

I hoped at least today he was looking out and seeing the monster elephant. After all, it was his quarrel that brought it here.

Makozi continued to gaze at the tower as we walked. "It's so much tall. It never used to be that tall." He turned to me. "Did the rain last night make it grow?"

I cocked my head. "I don't think so."

At length old Folorunso led us up to a short, squat wall with a square door. On the other side, I heard squealing and laughter, mixed with sing-song chanting.

Makozi grinned from ear to ear.

The door creaked open at the old man's touch, and we followed him into a sunny courtyard.

The space teemed with human children, bursting with life and energy. A cluster of boys chased each other through a grid of raised garden beds, while girls nearby laughed over a game that involved snatching pebbles from the ground. Another group of children linked arms and hopped up and down in a dizzying pattern.

It was like watching a hundred Makozis at once. I almost passed out.

Makozi turned to Old Folorunso, wide-eyed. "Are *they* all your sons?"

The old man laughed. "No, little man. I live here at the House of Mercy, and we run a school for boys and girls." He turned to me. "Most of the children here come from families who couldn't otherwise afford an education. We see to it they have the best training in math and reading and the sciences. I helped design the program, though now that I've retired I mostly handle the gardening. If you look here, that's where I plant melons, and over here ..."

Old Folorunso led us through the joyous chaos toward a red building, pointing out vegetables and calling greetings to various children as we went. As we passed through, I noticed some of the children stopped to stare—not at me, the mysterious robed stranger, but at Makozi. A few turned to whisper behind his back.

A sinking feeling filled my gut. Makozi's threadbare rags may have fit in at the docks, but here the children were neatly dressed, their tunics almost exclusively in reds and yellows with large geometric patterns. No one else wore orange with tiny shapes, and no one else was caked with dirt.

The school children's black hair grew close to their scalps, or it was braided or bound in orderly patterns—not the hodgepodge of messy locks my boy had.

Makozi didn't seem to have noticed the reactions, but I still felt that I had failed him in some way.

We approached the main building, decorated with glass panels in red, green, and blue. A set of wooden doors burst open, and out came several older women in plain grey dresses.

One held a tray piled high with white dough spheres, and two others lugged out a steaming pot, which they guided to a squat table. A fourth put down a stack of tin bowls. She grabbed a ladle and whacked one of them.

"Breakfast," she shouted over the din. "Get in your lines. Order, now."

The children cheered as they scrambled toward the table, somehow ending up in three neat queues. With practiced efficiency, the women dished up the soup and placed a dough sphere in each bowl. I caught a whiff of pungent spices and more of that sweet orange tuber.

"Thank you, Teacher," the children said as they received their bowls. They found places to sit along the fountain or garden walls, pinching off pieces of dough and sopping up the spicy broth.

I heard Makozi's stomach gurgle.

As the women served the last of the children in line, Old Folorunso stepped forward. "Two extra servings, sisters, for our guests."

The grey-clad women turned to us and gasped.

"He's *filthy*."

"Where did you find him—the drain?"

"Oh, his hair!"

Old Folorunso raised his hands. "Let me explain."

But the women pushed past him, surrounding Makozi, pinching at his hair and rubbing dirt off his face. I found myself jostled out of the way, unable to see my boy past the grey figures.

"This hasn't been combed in years—oh, there are twigs in here."

"Ay! I just saw a beetle. There, down by his ear."

"He's going to get parasites. How can a child this young even *have* hair this long?"

"Get the shears, Teacher Chioma. There's no saving it."

I let them fuss, my face burning with shame. I wasn't quite sure why—I'd returned him to the city the way I found him. I slunk toward the wall, not feeling like I should intervene. After all, they were human, and it was painfully clear I knew little about caring for their kind.

One of the women darted away from the cluster and returned a moment later with something shiny in her hands.

A knife.

"Magma!" Makozi wailed.

Something welled up inside me, hot and angry. I barreled toward the women, forcing them out of the way, and snatched my boy out of their reach.

Makozi clung to my arm, sniffling.

The women protested, reaching for my child again. I threw back my hood, tore off my veil, and raised my claws in warning. They drew back, one of them shrieking. I willed my fingers to glow, giving a blood-red hue to my claws.

"You no hurt my Kozi."

"Teachers." A stern voice boomed from the open door of the building. "What is the meaning of this?"

A stately woman appeared, dressed in a robe of grey so deep it was almost black. Her coiffed hair was silver and had been piled around her head like a crown.

"Headmistress Innosa," one of the women offered meekly. "We were merely trying to take care of this poor boy's matted hair."

The woman's dark eyes narrowed. "Against the wishes of his mother?"

"I not hims—" I started, but one of the women spoke over me.

"*That* is not his mother."

Mistress Innosa regarded me, and I extinguished my light and lowered my claws.

"She's his guardian at the very least," the regal woman said. "That much is obvious. And, as such, her wishes must be respected."

The women shuffled a little where they stood.

"Now," Mistress Innosa said to me, "If the boy is to be a pupil here, we do have grooming standards he must adhere to."

"Hims not here for pupil," I said. "Hims here for breakfast."

Old Folorunso stepped up and said something in her ear. Her eyes lit up. "Oh, so you're the one who rescued my dear brother. I should have known—word has spread through B'jeme about the mysterious goblin who saved a man's life."

Word spreading through the city was the last thing I wanted with the Faceless on my tail.

Mistress Innosa turned to the other women. "Teachers, please get this these two something to eat. And if you don't mind, I'd like to speak with you privately in my office afterward, Miss ...?"

"Magma." This time the name felt more natural than ever.

A little while later, Makozi and I sat in the headmistress' small office. The spice of the breakfast stew still tingled on my tongue.

The woman folded her dark hands and lay them on her desk. "I apologize for the over-eagerness of the teachers," she said. "We are well-meaning people, but still flawed. Now, what is the story about this raggedy child?"

"I finded him in woods," I said, purposely leaving out the parts about the fairy ring. No need to worry Makozi. "Hims say he from B'jeme, so I bringed him. We want to find hims mama today."

"I see." She glanced at Makozi's tangled mop of hair. "Is there a sentimental reason for resisting a haircut? I don't wish to intrude, but I would imagine it's quite uncomfortable for the child at this point."

I furrowed my brow, trying to understand. "You no can cut off part of my Kozi. Not hair, not fingers, not anything. I not let you hurt him. This is *flawed*."

"Wait. You don't think—" Mistress Innosa raised a black eyebrow. "Miss Magma, do you realize that cutting Makozi's hair will not cause him pain?"

Were his locks not just like any other part of his body?

A smile played on the woman's lips. "Well, this explains your reaction in the courtyard. But the fact is, trimming hair is like trimming fingernails—or claws, as might be in your case. It must be done periodically, and it's a painless process."

"Oh yeah," Makozi said. "I forgotted that."

Seriously?

I turned to him. "Kozi, you want hairs cut?"

The boy tapped his chin. "Would it make my head less hot and itchy?"

"Yes," Mistress Innosa said.

"Then probably, I guess so. Mama always cut my hair short."

"Very well. It may help your neighbors and family recognize you as you search for home. Do you know where you live, little one?"

"Seven Soldier Street, West Feather District."

"I not know where that is," I confessed.

"Nor do I, exactly," said Mistress Innosa, "but we can find a student from that part of the city who can lead you there. But first things first, Makozi. Let's get that hair cut."

Makozi was remarkably brave for a child having women shaving off parts of his body with a knife. For my part, I trembled so much that he had to reach down and hold *my* hand.

When the teachers finished, Makozi's remaining curls clung close to his head. He flashed a toothy smile.

He looked much better, I had to admit. But I blinked away

tears as the women swept away the mass of dirty hair that lay on the floor. What had gotten into me?

Mistress Innosa re-appeared, a tall girl in a pink robe trailing behind her. "This is Edara, from the West Feather District. She'll help you find your way." Mistress Innosa placed a hand on each of our shoulders. "I pray you have a successful search. And both of you are always welcome here at the House of Mercy."

I nodded my thanks.

The girl rocked from her tiptoes to her heels, eager to start. "Are you ready? Let's go to Soldier Street."

24

FATIMA

The tall schoolgirl led us through the maze of red buildings, her braided hair bouncing at her shoulders.

Makozi kept running his hands over his head, his tamed curls tight against his scalp. He grinned. "Mama will be so happy to see me. She will love to see my head."

I didn't speak, trying to memorize the contours of his face, the sparkle in his deep brown eyes, and the way he skipped and trotted over the red streets. If only I could push back the inevitable goodbye for just a little longer.

And yet at the same time we were walking too slowly. Shadows hung between buildings, and I kept watching for that indistinct outline to appear. I adjusted my veil for the twentieth time, trying to obscure my goblin features as much as possible.

"We're getting close," the schoolgirl announced. "It's a good thing it's been a long walk, because it means I've missed all of algebra now. If we keep it up, I'll miss textiles class, too. And look, there's the Three Old Soldiers."

She pointed to a street corner where three larger-than-life figures stood. The bronze men stood at attention, holding curved swords and wearing robes with many folds and sashes. I'd never seen anyone in B'jeme dressed like that.

"They represent three warriors from B'jeme's founding, though no one remembers their names now," she said as we approached the monument.

"Jamuike, Ayoola, and Hassan," said Makozi.

"Huh?"

Makozi pointed at the bronze figures, one at a time. "Jamuike, Ayoola, and Hassan. Mama told me it was important to remember."

"Are you making those names up?" the girl asked.

I shrugged. "Hims *does* make up names."

Makozi crossed his arms. "Mama said that's their names. It's written on their shoes."

"Don't be ridiculous." The girl leaned over the statue's pedestal and examined the first bronze foot. "Ayoola," she said slowly. "How did you know that? You're too little to read."

"Everybody knows Jamuike, Ayoola, and Hassan." Makozi wrapped his dark fingers around my hand and pulled me forward. "Come on, Magma. It's Soldier Street, and my house is number seven."

He ran ahead, dragging me behind him. I counted the brightly painted front doors in the block of buildings to our right.

One, two, three, four—here the street curved a bit, and Makozi urged me forward—five, six.

Makozi stopped in his tracks, and I stumbled into him.

No door seven.

There wasn't even a building here. Instead, water bubbled from a large fountain, and old men sat beside it, playing a game with pebbles arranged in a wooden tray.

"Where's my house?" Makozi's whole body trembled.

I turned to the schoolgirl. "This is Soldier Street?"

"Yes, the only one in the city."

Makozi's voice rose to a shriek. "Magma, where's my house?"

"Shh, Kozi," I said, gathering him into my arms.

He pushed at me, screaming. "Where's my house?"

"Shh." I stroked his short curls and he relaxed slightly, bawling into my cloak.

The old men stopped their game to look at us. I glared at them. "Where hims house?" I demanded.

One of them shrugged. "This fountain has been here for fifty years."

And indeed, the plaster at the base of the fountain had cracked and yellowed with age. What did it all mean?

Makozi continued to sob into my shoulder, soaking my red cloak with his tears. "Where's my house? Where's my mama?"

"We find them, Kozi," I said, not having the slightest idea how to do so.

"Ma'am," the schoolgirl offered, "we could try the Census Office. That's what the teachers do when a lost child shows up at the House of Mercy."

"Thems find lost houses?" I asked.

"Well, no. But they do keep track of everyone's names, and sometimes they can tell you where someone's moved to."

I lifted Makozi's chin and wiped his tears with my thumbs. "Kozi, we go to Senseless Office. Thems find you mama. No tears. We go now."

Makozi sniffed and clung to my hand. I turned to the school-girl. "You take us now?"

"Yay—I'll miss textiles class for sure."

Half an hour later, we stood inside a dusty old building, muggy with the mid-day heat. A man behind a tall desk peered down at us. "What do you children want?"

I cleared my throat behind my black veil. "This boy is lost. We need to find hims mama." I pointed to a pile of dusty scrolls beside him. "You find hims name in your books?"

He sighed and adjusted his spectacles. "What's the name?"

"Makozi Ibenwo," Makozi offered.

"Makozi, Makozi," the man muttered, sorting through the scrolls. "Not a name I've heard much of in current years—here we are."

He unrolled a scroll and examined the parchment for a minute. "Mako*zi*?"

"Yes," Kozi said, a tear stain still on his face.

"Hmm, we have no record of an Makozi Ibenwo."

He wasn't in the city's official book?

"Makozi Fatima," Makozi offered. "Fatima is my mama. I just remembered."

The man peered down at the scroll. "Huh." A cloud passed over his expression, then he shrugged. "No Makozi Fatima, either."

I crossed my arms. "You *huh*-ed."

"Pardon?"

"You say *huh*—you finded Fatima. Why you say no?"

The man sighed. "I did find an Makozi Fatima in our records —a young unmarried woman with no record of any child. But—"

"So yes," I interrupted, feeling a spark of hope. "This Kozi, hims a new person. Maybe him not get in your book yet. This Fatima, where hers house?"

"Nowhere," he said, his tone cool. "The only Makozi Fatima in our city went missing over seventy years ago."

My stomach dropped. I turned to the schoolgirl. "*What* number hims say?"

"Seventy, ma'am," the girl replied. "As in seven tens."

"Seven decades." The man rolled his eyes. "That is clearly not your Fatima. As far as B'jeme records go, your child and his mother do not exist. My only explanation is that you have the wrong city. Good day."

We stepped out onto the blazing red street, my head spinning.

Makozi clutched my hand. "But, Magma, where is Mama's house? Wasn't he gonna tell us?"

"Hims not know." I swallowed. "Kozi must be brave. We not find Mama today." Tears brimmed in his eyes, and I stroked his close-cropped hair. "Magma keeps looking."

He sniffled but somehow held it together.

I squeezed his hand. My brave boy.

"So ..." the schoolgirl said. "Um, back to the House of Mercy?"

I nodded absently.

The *wrong city*. All this work to get here, all that drama to get through the gate, and we'd come to the wrong place. That's what I got for taking directions from a five-year-old.

It explained why he knew nothing about stamps, had never seen Tajim's Wheel, and misremembered the height of the Mayor's tower. He wasn't from B'jeme.

But he knew the names written on the feet of the statue.

I bit a claw. We were no closer to finding Makozi's family than when I'd found him in the forest—only now I had zero clues to work with.

The schoolgirl led us back to the House of Mercy. This time the courtyard rang out not with children shouting and playing, but with song. The melody floated out from the main building, the children's high-pitched voices mellowed by the alto tones of their teachers.

"Hymns are almost done, so it's nearly time for lunch," the schoolgirl said. "Makozi, do you want to sit next to me when we eat? I'm sure the teachers won't mind."

Makozi looked back at me.

"It fine, Kozi. Eat. Magma need to think." He glanced at me once more, then he and the girl disappeared into the main building.

Meanwhile a song drifted out:

> *"May we love our brothers the way you love us.*
> *May we forgive others the way you forgive us."*

Something about the words resonated in me. I wished I could linger and listen to the whole song, but I had no time.

I paced among the garden beds.

What was I going to do? I could feel the Faceless' noose tighten around me. I had to get out of this city as fast as possible.

Taking Makozi back through the woods and searching for another city was much too risky. He was much safer here, with his own kind, and far from the heartless hunter that followed in my wake.

This was the House of Mercy, wasn't it? Perhaps I could explain Makozi's plight to Mistress Innosa. I reached down into my pocket and felt my cache of amethysts. *It will have to do.*

Tears burned in my eyes and I blinked them away.

"You know," said a voice behind me, "I'm looking for an assistant gardener."

Old Folorunso stood, leaning on a shovel.

"What?" I managed.

"If you and the boy want to stay here."

Oh, if only.

"It's the least we can do after you saved my life," the old man continued. "We have a boarding room to spare, and plenty of food. I'll even buy the boy an outfit to replace the old-fashioned tunic he has. Where did he find that relic, anyway?" Old Folorunso had begun his chatter mode again, and I began to tune him out. "No one's worn that shade of orange in decades, especially not with the pattern woven in the threads. My father had a woven-pattern tunic or two, but it was going out of fashion even then. And that was sixty-five years ago."

Wait, what?

"Sir, little boys not wear that now, but wear *seventy* years ago?"

"Sure," the old man said. "Sixty, seventy years, around that time. People of all ages wore woven patterns until someone invented the dye block. See, you carve a pattern onto wood, then apply the dye directly to—"

"Sir," I broke in, "you are old, yes?"

He chuckled. "You're not the first to observe that."

The wheels of my mind spun. Makozi knew the Soldier Street statue, but had never seen the fountain. He remembered the Mayor's tower being a different height. And when we first came around the corner of the city …

"Sir." My voice shook. "Before mans build giant wheel pump, what did B'jeme have at corner wall?"

Old Folorunso scratched his head. "Let's see, we had a series of monuments, but the corner was—oh yes, an elephant. A white one, made of plaster. It was taken down to make room for Tajim's Wheel, oh, I don't know, twenty-five years ago?"

But he's only five, my brain protested. *How could he—?*

"Elephants used to be a symbol of B'jeme," the old man continued. "Kind of funny now, considering. Perhaps this Zaraiyah has a sense of humor. Mind you, very few of us have seen a real elephant, and a traveler once informed us an elephant is grey, not white, and its tusks are short and straight, not the huge curved things our—"

"Asuka," I whispered.

"Pardon?"

I pushed past him toward the courtyard door. "Thank you, sir. Tell Kozi I back soon."

25

THE MAYOR OF B'JEME

My veil was coming undone, but I didn't stop to fix it. I dashed between colorfully dressed citizens, turning corner after corner of square red buildings and trying not to get lost.

I skidded to a stop. There, in the center of a busy throughway, stood the woman from my dreams—the one I could never catch up to. Her dark hair was cropped close to her head, and she brushed a wrinkle out of her faded red dress.

A chill ran down my spine. Now I knew why I recognized that red-and-gold pattern.

In the blink of an eye, she vanished.

I sprinted toward the docks. The enormous gate appeared before me, its keyhole shape creating a frame around the beast in the river. It blinked its pink eyes, dozing. I'd almost forgotten about the elephant within the complacent walls of B'jeme.

The guards in green nodded as I passed through the gates and scrambled down the stairway.

The Centrals had not forgotten the monster. A steady stream of people scurried toward the forest with their valuables bound in sacks, while others huddled in their ships.

At last I reached the sturdy house-boat. I beat on the door. "Asuka-san!"

The matron appeared, her greying hair escaping from her topknot.

"Asuka-san, what you know?"

The woman frowned. "About what?"

"Fairies."

Asuka ushered me inside the smoky interior, closing the door behind us. "What's wrong?"

I took a deep breath, trying to impose order on the thoughts tumbling through my mind. "My boy Kozi—hims remember elephant statue that is thrown away, but not Tajim's Wheel. Hims house has fountain on it, and fountain is old. Hims mama cuts hims hair short, but I finded him with hairs so long. And only lady with hims mama name is gone seventy years. What you know about fairies?"

Asuka poked at the small cooking-fire. "I've just heard stories. But they say the fairy dances don't work within mortal time."

"What that mean?"

"It means when you're within a fairy ring, what feels like a single night could last years in the real world."

I inhaled sharply. "Could last *seventy* years?"

"It's not unheard of."

I hadn't found the wrong city. I'd found the right city at the *wrong time*. I buried my face in my hands.

Seventy years too late. Everyone Makozi had known was either elderly or had passed away. And his mother—according to the Senseless Office, she'd never returned to the city.

I remembered the scrap of cloth I'd found in Woodshea—red and gold, just like the woman in my visions wore. It had been worn nearly to threads by decades of exposure.

"Kozi's mama, Fatima ... she dead." A sob shook me. After all we'd been through, our hope ended here, in failure and death. How was I going to tell Makozi? "She tried but never, never finded him."

"But *you* did," Asuka said. "You heard the Nomad brothers— no human could have located that fairy ring. It can't be helped. But you—you came along with your remarkable goblin senses. You found him and set him free. If it weren't for you, he'd still be their prisoner, maybe for a hundred more years. You've given the boy his life back, given him a future."

"But I not give him a mama." I stared at the cracked floor-boards. "Goblin cannot replace Fatima."

"Of course not, Magma-san. No one could. But right now, you're the best chance that boy has."

If only. Even if I wanted to stay and protect Makozi—and in my heart I did, more than anything—it couldn't be. If I didn't flee this city, the Faceless would find me and drag me back to the Pit. And where would that leave the child?

I dabbed at my tears with the corner of my Master's cloak. No time for regrets. I knew what I had to do.

"Thanks you for everything." I stood, reaching for my veil.

"Asuka-san!" The door flew open and Gangle tumbled in, panting. "Asuka-san, the mayor is gone."

Asuka shot to her feet. "What?"

"The city elders went to Olayo's tower." Gangle paused to wipe sweat from his forehead. "No one's heard anything from him since the elephant lady appeared. They forced open his door. His room was abandoned—papers scattered around, coin coffers empty. Olayo took his money and ran."

"Does Zaraiyah know this?" Asuka's voice trembled.

"Mareso's talking with her now. Come see."

We hurried after Gangle, pushing our way through the crowd that had gathered at the edge of the docks. I leapt onto a fishing boat and dug my claws into its mast, climbing up to get a better view.

Between the elephant's curved tusks bobbed a small rowboat. Mareso stood inside, looking up to the island-sized head.

The woman in blue stood on top, tapping her foot. "You

think you can rob me so easily?" Zaraiyah's voice boomed over the water.

"Please," Mareso said, "If we knew where the jewels were, we'd give them to you. But as I said, Olayo has fled and taken everything with him."

"You expect me to believe Olayo would stoop so low?" Zaraiyah put her fists on her hips. "No, I know his ploys when I see them. How much has he paid you to speak to me?"

"I'm not lying, I—"

Zaraiyah held up a hand. "Tell him he has until dawn. If the sun rises and I have not been repaid, this elephant will smash through your wall, trample your city, and tear down his tower."

"Eight thousand innocent people live here." Mareso moved forward as if to grab her feet. She flicked her scepter.

The elephant's pale trunk burst out of the water, striking the rowboat and flinging it through the air. Mareso landed in the river seconds before the hull smashed into the dock. A jagged piece of timber broke off on impact, flying into the crowd. A man cried out in pain.

Zaraiyah was not posturing.

Zaraiyah would crush us without remorse.

I had to get Makozi out of the city *now*.

"ORDER, ORDER!" The green-robed guards at B'jeme's gate shook their lances, trying to push back the throng of Centrals flooding the stairway. I clung to the bottommost stair, trying not to get trampled.

"Get back," the guard shouted. "Per an emergency declaration, there will be no entry for non-citizens."

"I just bought a stamp," a Nomad woman cried, holding out her wrist. "Let me in!"

"Stamps are no longer valid," the guard retorted. "Get back."

The crowd roared in protest. A crush of bodies shoved me onto the next stair. I found myself unable to get away, my Master's cloak pinned down beneath too many sandals. I wrenched it free, rolling off the stairway and onto the boards of the dock below.

Panting, I looked up to see the Centrals rushing the gate.

"*Back.*" Several more guards appeared, shoving men and women toward the stairs.

A metallic screech rang out over the shouting. A huge metal lattice plunged toward the ground, suspended on rusted chains. People pushed out of the way just as the iron spikes at the bottom of the grate hit the bricks with a *clang*.

The keyhole gate of B'jeme was now blocked by a cage-like portcullis. Centrals tried to squeeze themselves through the square openings between iron bars, but even from where I stood I could see this was futile. It was too narrow even for me.

I turned away, feeling sick. Stuck outside the gate once again, with Makozi trapped inside. How would I save him now?

26

THE BARRICADE

D ark clouds rolled in over the river, blood-red in the light of the setting sun. I stood beside Tajim's Wheel, trying to stay out of the way of panicking Centrals. Some had taken up throwing rocks and chairs at the gate's unyielding portcullis.

The huge elephant, white against the darkening river, shifted its weight and snorted through its trunk.

I paced along the boardwalk, trying to make sense of my options. If I left now, I might escape the Faceless, but I'd be leaving Makozi to the caprice of this mad Zaraiyah woman. She'd promised to trample the city on the way to the Mayor's tower— and the House of Mercy was right in her path.

My heart squeezed in my chest. I couldn't.

But there was only one way into the city beside the gate. And based on my encounter in the tunnels the last time, I had a good idea of who I might find there.

And when I lay paralyzed on a sled, what good would I be to Makozi then?

Two white-haired Rikeans in veils hurried past me. "I say let it crush them all," the first said to his friend. "Mareso and Egnatius are out of their minds if they think we're going to defend those ingrates."

My ears perked up. What was Mareso planning?

I fought my way through the chaos of the docks and found a crowd near the abandoned Market tents. Pushing my way between people and overturned furniture, I caught sight of Mareso's close-cropped black hair and goldenrod robe. Beside him were the Nomad brothers, Bare-Face and Hair-Face (or whatever their names were), plus a large centaur with golden curls and a gleaming white horse-coat.

It was the centaur who spoke, his four yellow hooves clomping as he paced the dock. "Who among us doesn't remember the names and faces of friends within those walls? It was Mayor Olayo who wronged us, not the people inside the walls. And Olayo's gone."

"But Egnatius," a copper-haired woman said. "They're the ones who let him do it."

"That is true." Egnatius tossed his golden tail. "Some of them got caught up in Olayo's greed and mean-spiritedness. But now he's fled like the coward he is, taking the treasure he promised them. He's left the people to be crushed to death for *his* crimes. Even if our old friends have been rude, they don't deserve that."

A murmur ran through the crowd.

A Tsuru man waved his hand dismissively. "They have their wall to hide behind."

"Yes," Mareso said, "And they're very confident that it will hold. But those of you who sell your goods beside the city wall know it tends to crumble under the slightest pressure. Imagine what it will do when that elephant takes his tusks to it."

Another murmur.

"What about Selena of Alavar?" a veiled Rikean asked. "She's supposed to protect us from these kinds of attacks."

"Even if the city elders were to send a message this moment," Egnatius said, "by the time Selena got here, she'd be too late. We have only until dawn."

"What we can do?" I heard my own voice say. "How we small peoples fight off huge elephant?"

Mareso caught my eye. "We don't," he said. "Once the elephant begins its attack, the city guards will come out to repel it. That's their duty. But if we can hold it back, we give them extra time and a fighting chance."

"So what we do is keep the monster away from B'jeme's walls." Egnatius clicked his hooves against the boardwalk. "We build a barricade."

"A barricade? With what?" a black-haired centaur demanded.

"With everything we have," Egnatius answered. "Our ships, our tent poles, our goods if needed—whatever we can put in the monster's way to keep it back."

"Are you mad?" asked a Tsuru merchant. "We're going bankrupt as it is. I'm out." He huffed away, and several others followed him.

"Look, that elephant is going to smash everything at sun-up anyway," Bare-Face said. "Why not smash things now and save some lives?"

"You can replace things," said Hair-Face. "But not one of us can replace a person."

"And," Mareso warned, "if the elephant breaks through one of those walls, it will kill people for sure."

Pain welled up inside me. "I stay, Mareso." I pushed my way to the front of the crowd. "I stay, I fight. I not let elephant smash my Kozi, or the childs at Foloso's school."

People in the crowd exchanged glances.

The woman from the ABC—the one with the fuchsia-dyed hands—appeared beside me. "My mother and I owe much to the kindness of the Faizan family. If I can do anything to spare their lives, I will."

"I will stand for Auntie Gbadamosi and her sons," a centaur with a black beard rumbled.

"I stand for the Kigabwo family."

"Naisha al-Tajir will not go unprotected."

A crowd of Centrals—just shy of a hundred—pressed in

toward Egnatius and Mareso. "Where do we start?" the woman with copper-red hair asked.

Egnatius squared his shoulders, a storm breeze rustling his curls. "As soon as the sun goes down, so that Zaraiyah can't see the details of our structure. Ready your lamps and torches."

NONE of us slept that night. In flickering firelight, we tore down every market tent and piled up poles, tables, crates, and barrels along the far side of the boardwalk. Rowboats and canoes were commandeered and broken down into planks, while larger vessels were anchored as close to the market strip as possible. The docks were now in such a jumble it would be impossible for anyone, let alone an elephant, to push through.

At least we hoped.

The barricade ended up being more of a pile than a wall, and stood only twelve feet tall at its highest point—far shorter than the red city wall behind it.

Our fortification's strength was uneven throughout, with the most difficult place to defend being around Tajim's Wheel at the corner of the city. We couldn't put anything so close that it would interfere with the wheel and piston mechanisms. Egnatius had us prop some boards around it to disguise the weak spot as much as we could.

"Keep it moving, kiddos," Gangle called from the top of a furniture pile. "No time for jilly-jallying." A wooden stool shifted beneath his foot and went tumbling into the river. "Whoops."

I set down the box I'd been carrying, frowning up at the mess.

"It not enough," I said aloud.

A slender young man in a silk turban looked at me, then turned away.

"It's tall enough to stop the beast," Hair-Face observed.

"Elephant is already taller than barricade," I said, "and hims not even standing all the way."

Hair-Face shrugged. "Doesn't have to be. Elephants can't jump, so it just has to reach above its knees. I think so, anyway."

No. The safety of our friends depended on this makeshift barricade holding up. It wouldn't do at all.

I marched toward the center of the market, where Mareso and Egnatius conferred with each other in low tones. From the looks on their faces, I guessed that they doubted the barricade's strength as well.

"Hey," I called. "I have soldier school."

Egnatius turned his golden head toward me. "Pardon?"

"In goblins land. I had soldier school."

The centaur raised an eyebrow. "You have military training?"

"That also." I pointed to the pile of planks and broken furniture. "Barricade, it need more."

"We've used everything at our disposal," Mareso said.

I shook my head. "You mans and centaurs, to you battle is all about strongness. But goblins, we small but we win, because we think sneaky."

"Ah, the goblins' famous cunning," Egnatius said. "Have you any 'think sneaky' ideas?"

"Yes. But we must hurry."

ASUKA SIGHED as Mareso and I stuffed her brightest-colored silks into crates. She ladled soup into the makeshift bowls that several exhausted Centrals held out to her.

"Magma-san," she said, "have you seen Etsuko?"

I felt a twinge of worry. "I not."

"When you do," Asuka said, her voice even, "remind her that I want her here, away from the barricade. I made that very clear."

I nodded, lifting my crate of silks and hauling it out of the houseboat. Mareso and I wove along the narrow path between the city wall and the barricade.

Two Rikeans approached us, their faces unveiled in the darkness and their white hair shining in the torchlight. One lifted a large vase, an elegant forest scene painted over its surface. "Where do these go again?"

"Spread through barricade," I said. "Find empty spots."

"All right," said the second Rikean, hoisting two clay pots beneath her arms.

We walked a little farther, passing a Tsuru merchant in what remained of a spice shop. "No, no, no," he scolded a handful of Centrals around him. "It took us months to get that shipment of cinnamon. Here, take the chili powder."

Mareso and I put down our crates of silks. The young man in the turban waited for us, his face obscured in the flickering light. He held out the ropes collected from sailing ships, and Mareso and I tied sections of silk along them, one every three feet.

"Lady Hobgoblin." Gangle appeared around a corner, hopping onto a broken table. "The centaur gang needs your help, at the old stamp tent."

Mareso nodded at me.

I rose. "Thanks you, Gangle."

A few minutes later I pushed through the green fabric doorway into the lamp-lit tent. Two burly Kavannan centaurs stood on either side, their huge forms blocking much of the light.

And there he was, leaning against the tent support pole.

The Faceless.

27

MARK OF PARDON

Time stopped. I could feel each beat of my heart pulsing at my throat, in my ears, behind my eyes.

The Faceless stood, his black mask pointed in my direction. He tensed a little when I entered—no doubt ready to pounce. But he didn't reach for his blowgun, not yet. His hands remained folded behind his back, his elbows at slightly awkward angles.

Stunned, I turned to the towering figures of the centaurs. Why would they betray me? How did they even know?

"Well?" The first centaur stroked the black braids in his beard. "You know him? We caught him crawling out of a hole in the city wall not far from here."

Wait. The centaurs *caught* him.

I looked at the Faceless again. His hands weren't folded behind his back—they were tied there, bound to the pole supporting the tent roof.

I exhaled.

The first centaur continued. "I think he's been hired by Zaraiyah to dig through the walls. You know, to make them weaker for when the elephant attacks. I wanted to crush him on the spot, but Chryses said we should hear his story first."

"It's only fair," the other centaur said. His dark beard looked as though it had only recently started coming in. "Problem is, he doesn't speak Vindorian. Or won't, at any rate. We pulled off his mask and saw he was a goblin, and Gangle suggested we talk to you."

I'd bet the Faceless loved that—having centaurs remove his sacred face covering.

"So," young Chryses continued, "I thought you could talk to him, tell us what he was really up to."

"Then we'll decide his fate," the first centaur rumbled.

My pulse quickened. The tables were turned. One word and I'd be free, never looking over my shoulder again.

The Faceless was at my mercy.

Trembling, I stepped closer to my persecutor. My tongue stuck to the roof of my mouth.

"Ah." His silky voice was calm. "I was wondering how they would kill me. This task befits a Blood Hand."

I ignored his comment. "Do you know why they've brought you here?" I asked in Goblin.

"Do not speak to me. I wish to die with my dignity intact."

I clenched my fists. Hadn't he said that showing mercy was immoral? If he wanted dignity, I'd let him suffer the justice he was so keen to dole out to others. All I had to do was tell the centaurs that yes, the drain pipe he'd come out of was in fact a work of sabotage, that he was Zaraiyah's lackey.

Let the centaurs crush him.

I opened my mouth, and suddenly I was back in Ipktu. The Slashers raised their wickedly sharp claws, prepared to give me the justice I had deserved.

Then I heard the Bandit King's voice: "Stop—she is sister."

I shook the vision away. This was different. The Faceless had refused me mercy. He didn't deserve any himself.

But who ever did? Certainly not me.

Also, there was the troubling detail that the Faceless wasn't guilty of the crime the centaurs accused him of. Traveling through the drain system was no threat to anyone but myself.

It would have been easier if the centaurs had asked no questions and done as they had planned. But now that I was involved, I had no choice.

"I know him." My hands trembled. "Hims not with Zaraiyah. Hole in wall from storm drain, not hims digging."

"I told you, Uncle Castor," said Chryses. The young centaur picked up a paintbrush and a jar of red pigment from the table. "Here. We'll give him a pardon stamp so the others know to leave him alone as well."

The older centaur drew a knife from his belt. The Faceless cringed.

With a slice, the ropes that bound the Faceless to the pole fell away. Chryses pulled the Faceless' arm toward himself, peeling back one of the black sleeves. The spiral of burn scars gleamed in the torchlight.

The centaur grimaced. "Ugh, this one's been through a lot, hasn't he?"

The Faceless tried to pull his arm away, but the giant centaur didn't even notice his resistance.

"Stop," I said in Goblin. "They're releasing you. They're going to give you a mark of pardon and let you go."

"Why?"

"They accused you of a crime you didn't commit, and I told them to let you free." I swallowed. "Besides, I swore never to harm another goblin as long as I live. I intend to keep that oath."

The Faceless froze, though whether the expression behind the mask was one of thanks or disgust, I'd never know.

"Let's see," Chryses said, dipping the stamp into the pigment. "Here's a clear spot."

And a moment later, a series of squiggles covered an unscarred portion of his arm.

The exact space where the badge for my capture was supposed to go.

"I'll write your name on him, Magma, since you're the one who pardoned him, and the people on the barricade respect you."

Chryses made a series of additional marks with a paintbrush and released the scarred arm. "You're free to go."

The Faceless drew back, staring at the pigment. Then he turned his blank mask toward me. "I'd rather you'd let them kill me."

"Clear out." I tried to steady my voice. "Before they change their minds."

He slunk toward the tent's doorway, pausing for a moment to look back at me. I felt a wave of nausea, half-expecting him to pull out his blowgun then and there.

Instead the curtain rustled once, and he melted into the shadows.

28

SONG AND BANNER

For the rest of the night my neck prickled. I was certain the Faceless lurked in the barricade's jumble of shadows, biding his time before he took aim. I helped Mareso and the others set the vases and baskets of spices in place, never speaking a word.

About an hour before dawn, the dark skies opened up, pouring rain down on us and our mess of a barricade. The Centrals and I huddled beneath any shelter we could find, our clothing soaked through.

The clouds slowly became distinguishable above the treeline —a dull iron against the leafy silhouettes.

Dawn.

I turned to the gate of B'jeme, expecting to see the green-clad city guard lined up and ready to defend the city.

Instead, huge planks of wood stood flush against the portcullis, creating an impassable door.

Sometime during the night, while we labored to build a fortress to protect their city, they had come and shut us out.

"We are abandoned," the young man in the turban said, bowing his head. "They've left us out here to die."

The city guards had backed out, relying wholly on the city

wall—the earthen wall that even now grew slick and soft in the rain.

"Egnatius, it's over." Castor, the dark-bearded centaur, stomped forward on heavy hooves. "If their own city guard won't defend them, why should we?"

"Please." Egnatius' blue eyes implored behind his wet curls. "Doubtless this is a poor choice a few officials have made. We can't condemn the rest of the population to—"

"Look at us." Castor motioned toward our rag-tag group of Centrals. "We aren't warriors. We're middle-aged merchants and second-rate sailors. Our hearts were in the right place, but without the guard, we don't stand a chance. Not one of us signed up for certain death. It's over."

Egnatius closed his eyes and bowed his head.

For a terrible moment, our band of Centrals stood in the grey rain. Even Gangle kept silent, water dripping from his multi-colored tunic. Then a few of the Rikeans lowered their veils and turned toward the woods.

Panic tore through me. Zaraiyah and her monster would arise at any moment. Perhaps our barricade would slow them, and perhaps not. Without the traps, the wall would be breached within the hour. By noon, hundreds of homes and their inhabitants would lay crushed in the aftermath.

How could we just do nothing?

As Centrals gathered their belongings and walked away from the barricade, a primal scream welled up inside me. I tried to redirect it, and found myself wailing out the words of my lullaby.

> *"There is a boy,*
> *Hims eyes are brown,*
> *Hims hairs are black,*
> *Hims name is Kozi."*

I'd composed another verse I'd meant to share with him, and

now would never have the chance. I took a shaking breath and sang:

"A goblin there,
She keeps that boy,
She loves that boy,
She loves that Kozi.

Tears ran down my cheeks in the rain.

"Oh bring the stones
The grave-top stones
Where children lay.
Place stones on Kozi."

I buried my face in my hands, not caring if the whole band saw me sob.

Pull yourself together, Valshara. You've got a barricade to defend.

No matter what the others chose, my place was here, giving whatever strength I had left to protect my child.

Wiping tears from my eyes, I rose.

Mareso stood before me. Around us stood a small group of Centrals—perhaps fifty in number.

Fuchsia stepped forward. "We won't let them die, Magma. There are children in there, and kind old women, and people who have cared for us over the years. If there's anything we can do to change their fate, we will do it."

Bare-Face nodded. "Let us show that even if the people abandon us, we will not abandon the people of B'jeme."

A deep rumble shook the boards beneath our feet. We rushed to the barricade, climbing up furniture to peer over the top.

Zaraiyah stood on the elephant's head, her blue scepter in her hand. The creature flapped its ears and thrashed its long snout, letting out a deafening sound like a trumpet blast.

"What is this you have done, foolish ones?" Zaraiyah called. "Broken boats, scraps of wood? Did you really think this will slow us down?"

She raised her arms, and the monster beneath her rose, river waves heaving with its movement. Four enormous legs appeared beneath the pendulous body, each wider around than several tree trunks.

Remarkably similar to the "relevant leg" Makozi showed me in the forest. How many people could it crush with each step?

At last the white elephant stood at full height, uttering a low rumble as menacing as a growl. Even standing on the river bottom, it towered over our barricade. If it stretched out its serpentine snout, it could easily reach the top of B'jeme's wall. Raindrops ran down its twenty-foot tusks.

The young man beside me shook. I glanced at my own hands to see my fingers flickering red. I hadn't lost control of my phosphorescence since I was a frightened child.

Zaraiyah looked down on us from her lofty vantage point. I was glad for the tangle of ships between her and us.

"Wave a white flag of surrender and I will give you half an hour to evacuate." Zaraiyah sounded bored. "I have no quarrel with you, scattered nations of Vindor."

"You have no quarrel with the people of B'jeme either," Egnatius called, stomping a hoof against the overturned cart he stood upon. "Olayo has fled—why kill innocent people?"

"I'm growing impatient, Docklings. Surrender now."

I clenched my teeth.

"I said *now*."

Our little band of Centrals held our ground.

"Then you will die first." Zaraiyah waved her scepter forward, and the elephant stomped toward the docks. With a swing of its tusks, it took out the first boat it encountered—a sleek black dhow that skidded over the nearest pier and splintered to pieces.

So this was the beginning. And very possibly, the ending.

How strange to think that after all I'd risked to escape the Pit,

I was willing to throw my life away here, outside a human city that days ago I hadn't known existed.

But nothing would move me from this spot.

Zaraiyah swung her scepter again, and the elephant hooked its tusks beneath a section of pier. A moment later it ripped the structure out of the water, sending logs flying into the air. Wood struck nearby ships with ear-splitting cracks. One knocked the curled bowsprit clean off of massive trade vessel, which immediately swamped with river water and sank.

My red lights flickered again. Did we really think our pile of chairs and tables had a chance?

"Steady," Egnatius called.

I took a breath and clung to the nearest scrap of wood.

Zaraiyah's elephant tore a path through the crowded piers, moving at an angle toward the corner of the city.

"Egnatius," one of the dark-haired centaurs bellowed. "It's headed for the wheel."

No. The wheel was our most vulnerable spot, and had none of my traps. Like an idiot I'd just assumed the beast would aim for the gate.

We had to do something, fast.

I scrambled up and over the barricade wall, slipping on a loose plank, and leapt onto an abandoned sailing ship. Digging my claws into its mast, I climbed up the rigging and scaled it until I reached the crow's nest. The vessel bobbed underneath me in a very disconcerting way.

"Hey," I yelled. The rain had stopped temporarily, allowing my voice to carry. "Hey, you elephant—what that ugly thing on you head?"

Even from a hundred feet away, I saw the woman in blue stiffen. She turned my direction.

Got her.

I slipped off my red cloak and waved it in the air. "Over here, elephant. What that ugly hat you have? Oh, it not a hat. It a brat."

"Magma," Mareso whispered from his spot on the barricade. "What are you doing?"

If this woman had an ego big enough to destroy a city over a personal quarrel, then she wouldn't let an insult go, either.

"How dare you?" Zaraiyah's voice boomed. She raised her blue scepter, and the elephant stopped moving mid-stomp. Zaraiyah swirled the rod in a semi-circle, and the monster turned around and began smashing its way toward me.

I realized then that with Zaraiyah standing toward the back of its head, the huge creature's eyes couldn't detect the movements of the scepter. How did it obey so efficiently?

"Big elephant, why you listen to lady? She worse than goblins' brat. She say '*waaaaah,* me want shiny rocks.'"

Zaraiyah's dark eyes burned. "Who do you think you are?"

I cringed as the elephant tore up another section of pier, crashing toward me. "Me? I goblin that more smart than brat. When they say Mayor leaved, goblin knows what those words mean. Brat need goblin to teach Vindorian? I very more good than you."

I could see the elephant's pink eyes now, and the wrinkles along its serpentine snout. It used the thumb-like ends to lift a rowboat from the water.

The vessel flew my direction, just missing the mast I clung to, but hitting the barricade with a thud.

Debris clattered down its edges and a woman screamed.

"Steady," Egnatius cried.

I turned once again to Zaraiyah, steeling myself. For a moment I saw a small sparkle of blue high up on the monster's forehead. It was a jewel no bigger than my hand, glowing with a soft light.

With Zaraiyah so close to me now, I didn't need to shout, but I didn't lower my volume. "Brat smash mans, and ladies, and childs, and babies. But when you get to tower, you say 'waaah, Mayor not here? Why no one tell me? *Waaaah!*"

The elephant's foot crunched through another section of the pier.

Just a little closer and we'd have them.

I grabbed my red cloak and waved it tauntingly. "You want flag? We not give you white flag. Our flag *red*."

Zaraiyah screeched and waved her scepter again. The blue stone at the end gave a small flash of light, and the creature's serpentine snout whipped toward me. My nostrils burned with that white-hot magic smell.

With watering eyes, I spun around the mast and leapt toward the barricade below. I landed hard on an old door and scrambled over the maze of broken furniture. I found a protruding pole and hooked the end of my cloak over it. The red fabric flapped in the storm breeze.

"You want flag? Come and get."

The elephant took another splintering step, now mere yards from the barricade.

"NOW," Egnatius shouted from below.

The air ricocheted with a deafening crash. Fifty clay urns smashed simultaneously, just as a hundred silk flags flew skyward in an explosion of color. I managed to scramble down into the shelter of the barricade for the third part of the attack—spice bombs that launched into the air, filling the sky with burning clouds of chili powder and black pepper.

The elephant reared backward, flapping its ears. It made a garbled trumpet sound as it rubbed the end of its peppered snout into its pink eyes—then let out a guttural roar.

The creature whirled around. The boat mast I'd been perched on only a minute before crashed toward the water as the monster's back end jarred the barricade, knocking down a whole section.

"You stupid beast." Zaraiyah swung her scepter in a circle, and the elephant beneath her jerked. The lady in blue stumbled and lost her balance. She fell, hitting the water with a splash as the elephant beat a hasty retreat through the maze of ships.

"Yeah, get out of here, you white lump!" Gangle shouted, waving his arms.

Cheers rang out. Egnatius leapt on top of the barricade, his hooves clattering against loose wood. "Did anyone see where Zaraiyah fell?"

"I see her," a Nomad called.

"You two there," Egnatius ordered. "Go pull her out and bring her to me. Don't let her get away."

I peered over the top of the barricade, my eyes stinging with a stray wisp of pepper. The monster splashed downriver, using its trunk to spray its eyes with water.

We'd done it. We'd actually done it.

I turned and leaned against a barrel, gazing at at B'jeme's wall —untouched. Kozi and his friends were safe. Gratitude overwhelmed me.

"Magma!"

The panicking voice was that of Hair-Face. I scrambled down to the market street. "I here."

He motioned for me to follow. "She's hurt. Bad."

My voice trembled. "Who hurt?"

I followed him through the narrow space between the wall and the barricade, to the section that had collapsed during the attack.

Mareso kneeled, a figure cradled in his arms with a damp and bloody shirt.

I recognized the young man in the turban—only now the turban had fallen away to reveal a lock of long brown hair.

Etsuko.

29

THE BELLY OF B'JEME

"Etsuko!" I rushed to her, using my claws to slash away her reddening clothing. I had to find her wound, stop the bleeding.

Mareso cradled her head, a tear running down his dark cheek. "You weren't supposed to be here."

Etsuko gazed up at him, a faint smile playing on her pale lips. "I wanted to do you good. And I did, didn't I? I pushed you out of the way when the wall fell. The table and mirror would have landed on you, but it fell on me instead."

A crowd of Centrals gathered. A Rikean woman in white leaned beside me, examining Etsuko's bleeding torso. "Blunt force trauma, and a glass shard," she said. "Goodness, it's sharp as a knife, and embedded deep."

I reached forward. "We take out."

The woman grabbed my hand. "No. It's blocking the blood flow. If we remove it now, she'll die in minutes. We need a surgeon."

"You not sturgeon?" I asked.

The Rikean shook her head. "I don't believe anyone out here is. We have to get her into the city."

"And how do you propose that?" rumbled Castor the centaur,

crossing his burly arms. "If you haven't forgotten, the city guards have blocked off the only way in."

I furrowed my brow. Not the *only* way in.

Etsuko reached up and touched Mareso's thin beard, her fingers trembling. "By the way, Mareso, I believe that I was a little bit in love with you." Her eyes fluttered closed.

"Etsuko, no," I cried. "You not end here."

She gave a rattling breath but did not open her eyes.

I looked up at Castor's towering figure. "Where you see all-black goblin come through wall?"

"Not too far from the stamp tent. Why?"

I peeled off my black silk dress—the one Etsuko had given me—and thrust it into the doctor's hands. "Wrap her tight. Attach rope I can pull. I get Etsuko inside the city."

"How?" she asked.

"Tunnels under streets."

Mareso looked up in alarm. "You don't mean to drag her through the *drains*?"

"You know other way?" I wiped my bloody hand on my linen trousers and grabbed a rope dangling from a mast.

Mareso bit his lip. "But it's so cramped and dark."

"I goblin. I like cramped dark. Now hurry."

A few minutes later, Etsuko lay on a thick wool blanket, a harness of rope gently tied around her chest and legs. Layers of black silk were wound around her bleeding torso in an attempt to stabilize the glass shard. I grabbed the rope and slid her feet-first toward the opening in the wall.

Etsuko was so slight that her reclined body would fit through any of the main passages. She'd be okay so long as I didn't get lost in the maze. Unfortunately, I hadn't gotten far on my initial reconnaissance trip.

The Rikean doctor frowned at Etsuko's bloody silks. "Whatever you do, don't let the glass get knocked or jostled," she said. "Another internal cut would be fatal. She doesn't have long as it is. Don't dawdle."

Etsuko groaned and her eyes fluttered once.

"Find the main city square, if you can," Mareso said. "There's a hospital close by that the citizens can take her to."

I crawled into the mouth of the tunnel, the world going peaceful and dark around me. Silhouetted in the daylight behind me, Mareso and the Rikean guided the blanket and its precious load into the opening.

Mareso paused for a moment, kissing Etsuko's clammy forehead.

"Hang on, Etsuko."

The transition from midmorning to midnight was instantaneous. I flashed my red light ahead of me to orient myself. The clay tunnel angled down sharply, but was mostly dry. Somewhere beyond the walls came the whoosh of water and the rhythmic groans of Tajim's Wheel at work.

I put my shoulder to the rope and dragged Etsuko into the descending pipe. Once again, I heard uneven breathing against the mechanical hum, but this time it was Etsuko's rattle. As long as I could hear that I would continue.

After a minute the clay pipe leveled out. Every hundred feet or so, a shaft of daylight illuminated the tunnel from above. These were the street-level openings, covered with clay grates that allowed rain to fall through.

We were under the city streets. I'd need to find a ladder in order to climb out.

My body shivered as I dragged my dying friend from light shaft to light shaft. In the past twenty-four hours I'd had no sleep, no food, and a pendulum of emotions: gut-wrenching terror for Makozi, the euphoria of victory, and the shock of seeing my first friend bleeding to death.

Focus, Valshara. I took a deep breath, listening to the rhythmic clicks and whooshes all around me.

Etsuko moaned and went quiet. I froze. An agonizing moment later, the rattle returned and she breathed again.

How much longer until the center of the city?

The next shaft of light poured down about twenty feet above me. An impenetrable shadow swallowed the light before it reached the bottom of the pipe.

I blinked and the shadow was gone. My fatigue was wreaking havoc on my senses.

I dragged Etsuko through the illuminated spot, the only shadows cast being our own. A glance upward revealed a ladder in the side of the shaft toward the street opening. Could this be far enough into the city?

There was one way to find out.

I let go of Etsuko's rope and tensed my muscles, preparing to jump. But before I could move, a finger brushed the back of my shoulder.

Then claws dug into my arm.

"Well." The word was in Goblin, spoken by a voice that turned my blood ice-cold. "One-Eight-Six-Two. Have you come to me, then?"

I whirled around and found myself staring into a black abyss —the mask of my enemy. My stomach dropped. *Not now.*

"Please." I tried to pull away from his grasp. "Give me one hour. It's a matter of life and death."

He dug his claws in deeper. "If you wish to dump your corpse, here's as good a place as any. No one comes down here."

I blinked, trying to understand his meaning. "I haven't killed her. I'm trying to save her life."

Etsuko gasped from her place on the floor of the pipe, her breath gurgling. The Faceless glanced in her direction, possibly surprised that she was in fact alive.

But not for much longer.

"Please. She'll die if I don't get her to a doctor. Let me go, just for an hour. Then you can dispose of me as you see fit."

"Even you understand why that would be foolish. Especially after I've chased you halfway across the Topside world."

I grabbed the Faceless' gloved hand. He pulled away, startled.

"You've caught me, fair and square," I said. "I'll surrender, I promise, but first grant me this one favor."

"Why should I grant a Blood Hand a favor?"

"Because I spared your life."

For a moment the only sound was the churning of the wheel mechanism.

"That"—the Faceless shook his head—"that doesn't change the fact that you have a criminal past to answer for."

"No, but it does put you in my debt."

The masked lips stayed silent for a moment. "You have until the sun is directly overhead. One minute more and I'll be compelled to shoot you in the street."

"Understood." Grabbing Etsuko's rope, I pulled her through the tunnel, praying this delay wouldn't prove fatal.

"One more thing," the Faceless said behind me.

I cringed.

"Take the left pipe there," he said. "It opens up into a chamber with a stairway. It will be easier to get her up that way than with the ladders."

"Uh—thank you."

Etsuko and I moved down the tunnel the Faceless had indicated. I squinted, watching for a trap. But just as he'd said, the tunnel led to a large chamber. And there, against the curved wall, stood an honest-to-goodness stairway, rising to street level.

I dropped Etsuko's rope and clambered up the stairs. Shafts of weak sunlight poured down from the street above. The opening was blocked by a heavy clay circle, dotted with small holes. I grunted as I lifted the cover, then climbed my way up onto the street.

The sandaled feet of a dozen B'jeme citizens walked past me. "Help!" I cried.

The people around me startled and pointed. How disconcerting it must be to see a mud-stained goblin climbing out of the drain.

"Please, anybody, help. I need sturgeon—my friend dying."

"What's that you say?" an older man said, leaning closer to me.

I pointed down through the manhole. "My friend down there. She hurt on the barricade, and she die if no doctor come."

The old man pointed at people in the crowd. "You, go fetch Doctor Tolibae. You two, help get the patient up."

"From the storm drain? How?"

"Stairs are here," I said.

A moment later, two young men carried Etsuko up the narrow stairway and toward the daylight.

I paced above them at the opening. "Careful—she have glass. Do not bump her. Oh, watch careful."

They laid her down upon the red mud of the street. Her face was pale as the moon, her breathing frightfully shallow.

"She's a Central," an old woman observed. "What was it you said about a barricade?"

I grasped Etsuko's chilly hand and put my other palm against her cheek. "Last night, Centrals builded barricade to protect B'jeme wall."

"But the guards told us the wall is all we need," a young man said. "It's stood for—"

A trumpet blast from the river cut his sentence short. The citizens glanced at each other, fear in their eyes.

"You see elephant tusks?" I asked. "You wall of mud not can stand. So Centrals build barricade. Elephant very strong and break docks, but we scared him away. But hims crush part of barricade, and Etsuko hurt."

A murmur ran through the crowd. "The Centrals are protecting us?"

"They're dying, while we cower here."

A man in a cream robe elbowed his way through the crowd. "I'm here. Where is the patient?" He glanced down at Etsuko. I was still new to reading human expressions, but the way his lips tightened filled me with dread.

I pointed to the soaked silk bandages. "She has glass there. We not take out because it make her die more."

The man in cream turned to a woman beside him. "Prepare a room. Sanitize my surgical tools. Hurry."

He motioned to the young men.

I squeezed Etsuko's clammy hand as they lifted her. "My friend. Please, my friend, hold on." Her limp fingers brushed against mine, and then they rushed her down the street behind the doctor.

A ray of sunshine broke through the clouds above. My shadow appeared, stretching over the cobblestones before me.

"Hey," I asked an old woman beside me. "Where House of Mercy?"

"Up that road and a block to the left. Why?"

I turned without answering, racing through the streets. Perhaps I had time to make one more thing right.

30

ALL THE DAYS EVER

I burst through the courtyard doors of the House of Mercy, weaving my way through clusters of children. It took all my willpower not to make eye contact with any of them, not to pick out the little face I loved the most.

It was better this way.

I rushed up to Mistress Innosa's door and barged in without knocking. Behind a rickety desk, the matron looked up from a scroll.

"Magma—we've been looking everywhere for you."

I slammed the door behind me and dug into my pockets. A moment later, three handfuls of amethysts—every one I had—lay on top of Innosa's scroll.

She gasped.

"These all for Kozi. For hims school. For hims food. For hims … home."

"This would more than pay for his entire education." Mistress Innosa looked up at me, her dark eyes concerned. "You're not leaving him?"

I pointed to the temporary stamp on my wrist. "Time is up. I not can stay."

"Surely we can do something, Magma. No one can love that boy as much as you do."

My throat tightened. "Please try."

"I don't know if the teachers have said something to you, but Makozi belongs with you."

"Hims not can come with me." She might as well know the truth. "I runned away from goblins caves. I finded Kozi by mistakes and bringed him here. Now a goblin guard is here. He takes me back to caves, I not can say no. Hims waiting now." I hung my head, a tear splashing on the brick floor. "Makozi, hims family dead. When I go away, he has nobody but House of Mercy. Please."

Mistress Innosa paused for a moment in thought. "This goblin guard," she asked, "is he sent by—?"

Before she could finish, the door swung open and banged against the wall. "Magma!"

I spun around. Makozi ran to me and I wrapped my arms around him. I'd meant to avoid this moment, thinking it would be too painful. But it was worth it just to hold him one more time, to memorize the feel of his soft cheek against mine, to inhale that human odor I'd come to love.

"Kozi. You happy with other boys, girls?"

"Yeah, they're really nice. Well, except some of the boys won't let me play Jump-Stones. They say I'm too little, but I'm big. You know I'm big."

"So big. And smart." I swallowed hard. "Magma says goodbye now."

"Goodbye?" His eyes narrowed. "When you're coming back?"

I paused, feeling like I was at the edge of a cliff. "I ... I not, Kozi. I bringed you here, to a place where a boy can be happy. But now I must go ... home. To caves."

"*I'll* go to the caves."

"No. Thems too bad and scary. Not a place for my Kozi. Hims stay here and be happy."

"I won't." He stomped his foot. "Do not leave, Magma. Stay with me."

"Oh, I wish, Kozi. More than any wish ever. But it not can happen."

"But ..." His little voice broke. "I very, very love you. I love you all day."

I choked back emotion. "Magma and Kozi, they never forget each other. Always love each other, from far away. Every day."

"Magma." Mistress Innosa's voice jolted me back to the outside world.

Where was the sun? How many minutes did I have left?

"I go now." I wanted *this* to be our last memory together, not him watching me get knocked unconscious with a dart and dragged away. Makozi grabbed my hand, and I was forced to shake him away. He burst into tears.

Mistress Innosa moved forward to take my arm. "Magma, wait."

I dodged her and ran for the door, stealing one last glance at my boy, a lost child wailing in the center of the room.

"Kozi, I love you all the days ever."

And I fled.

I RAN through the muddy streets, skirting buildings and dodging the sandaled feet of citizens. My shadow glided beneath me. I'd overstayed my time.

My heart hurt so much I felt it as physical pain. To leave behind the little boy I loved was harder than my whole six years in the Pit.

But I was leaving him far better off than I'd found him. For seventy years, he'd been stuck as the fairies' plaything, invisible to all human eyes. Only a straying goblin could sniff him out and save him.

I turned the corner and entered the city center, the drain cover still pulled up. People milled about, but I couldn't identify any of the kind strangers who'd helped rescue Etsuko.

I swung myself into the drain-hole, plunging into the cool blackness beneath the street and taking the stairs three at a time.

Makozi was safe and provided for, in a joyous house full of people I knew would love him. And his city was no longer under attack.

So what if I'd lost my freedom making that happen? The exchange had been more than worth it. Besides, my freedom had only ever been temporary. No one actually escaped the Faceless, not in the end. Instead of spending my brief liberty mindlessly running, I'd come alive in a way I never had before.

I slowed, making my way through the clay pipe to where I knew the Faceless waited.

Fate required that I return to the Pit. But the Pit's sufferings could no longer drive me to despair. Memories of Makozi would lighten my load, his laughter ringing in my ears and his face brightening the gloom. In snatches of sleep I would dream about him. In my suffering I would wonder about the delightful young man he would grow into, knowing he was safe and cared for.

His love would give me light for the rest of my dark days.

I approached the place of my capture, the shaft of light from above illuminating the dusty pipe floor. My feet grew heavier with each step.

"I'm here," I whispered, stepping into the circle.

31

SHACKLES

For a moment I stood alone. Then a soft voice said, "Stop there." It came from behind, from the pipe I'd just passed through.

The Faceless had been following me. Of course—he wouldn't have let me out of his sight. Which means he would have been able to tranquilize me the moment I missed my deadline. Why hadn't he?

The light in the circle around me diminished as his black form approached. I straightened, bracing for his needle.

He twisted the blowgun between his black fingers, but did not raise it.

"Walk." He indicated a tunnel to our left, and I obeyed, hearing his footfalls close behind me. There was nowhere to run, and no point in trying with his weapon at the ready. I wondered how long I'd be able to walk through the free world before being tranquilized and waking up again in the Pit. I hoped at least to see one more sunset. The preposterous colors had grown on me.

"You went a second place," he said at length.

"I didn't mean to be late."

"Who was the child?"

My muscles tensed, and even now I felt the need to protect Makozi. "Wh-what child?"

"The one who wailed for you."

He'd seen. Somewhere in the shadows, the Faceless had coldly observed one of the worst moments of my life.

"I found him in the forest," I said. "He was being held prisoner, and I bought his freedom. He came from B'jeme, so I brought him here to find his family."

"Wait. That's why we came all this way? So you could help a random scatterling?"

I set my jaw and said nothing. How could the Faceless understand?

"Who was the injured girl?"

"My friend." A pang of worry. "She was hurt on the barricade and she needed a city doctor."

We stepped through another confluence, and he directed me to the rightmost tunnel. In the darkness around us, the mechanisms of Tajim's Wheel whooshed and clicked.

"Did you know, One-Eight-Six-Two, that you might have gotten away? I was certain you'd fled after our ..."—he paused for half a second—"encounter. I'd already chosen a forest path to pursue you down. But then you took that girl through the drains, even though you knew I was here. Why?"

"It was the only way," I said. "I'd do it all again."

"You would knowingly send yourself back to the Pit?" He sounded confused. "Just to help some Lowblood human?"

"Isn't there anyone *you* love?"

The Faceless said nothing as we headed down the narrow tunnel. I almost tripped on the downward-tilting floor. We were heading away from the city center and back toward the river.

Finally he murmured, "I have a wife."

I wasn't expecting that somehow. "Well, if you had the power to save her life, wouldn't you do it? No matter what it cost?"

"Of course not." He stiffened for a moment, as though his

confession had shocked him as well. He lost his footing on the clay incline and stumbled.

"I don't mean that I would just ..." He paused. "I mean, it would be inappropriate. She's my subordinate, and it's not proper for someone of my standing to ..."

I shouldn't have been surprised. Of course a Guidelight would be heartless at his core. The whole lifestyle was ruthlessly self-centered: performing rituals of "righteousness" for the sole purpose of earning badges. Every burn mark on his arm increased his prestige, and moral prestige was everything.

But at the same time, each scar represented physical abuse that he'd been conditioned to seek out. He'd spend his entire life compelled to do more, to prove his worth over and over, all while the abuse ran rampant.

The Guidelight philosophy was pitiless toward the rest of society, I realized, but downright cruel to its own adherents.

As much as I wanted to despise the Faceless, who was I to condemn him? For years my greatest aspiration had been to rain down pain and vengeance on anyone in my path.

But at least those of us in the Pit knew we were prisoners.

"I know what you're thinking," the Faceless said, breaking the silence.

"You do?"

"You think that your bleeding heart somehow redeems you, that love is more important than sacrifice. But how could that be?" His voice rose. "It's about hard work and moral excellence. Things like the Rite of Recitation, which I've done *twice*. Eating pure foods, wearing the mourning robes, sacrificing my own flesh. What good is sentimentality when compared to *this*?"

The Faceless pulled back his sleeve to reveal his armful of scars. And there, plainly visible in a shaft of light from above, was the Mark of Pardon that had saved his life.

My name inked into his skin.

For a moment the only sound was that of Tajim's Wheel. Finally, the Faceless lowered his arm.

"Go."

"Are you—" I didn't dare breathe. "Are you letting me free?"

He said nothing, and I noticed the fingers of his other hand fiddling with the blowgun. What was going on behind that blank mask?

"Do you mean," I asked cautiously, "if I walk away right now, you won't come back after me? That you promise mercy?"

"Mercy." He turned to me, sharply. "That's the root of it all, isn't it? Mercy. The whole earth crumbles before it. If a criminal like you can be forgiven, does that put you on the same plane as the righteous?" The black fingers tightened around his weapon. "If so, what's the point of laboring to do good? Who will praise us if we end up on the same level as convict slaves? It's not *fair*."

He jammed his blowgun into a hidden pocket of his tunic and drew out an object wrapped in black cloth.

With his other hand he grabbed my wrist, his fingers shaking.

"Have the Guidelights labored for nothing? Hasn't our pain earned us a place among the stars?"

The cloth fell away, revealing two iron shackles. Between them stretched three feet of spider cord.

"It's mercy that ruins everything, that throws the whole world's system into disarray. A Blood Hand does good and a Guidelight must learn from her? It's outrageous."

Wrenching my arm, he forced my wrist into the metal ring, right where my old chain had been. I tried to pull away, but he held tightly, his claws digging deep. He slammed the shackle closed with far more force than needed.

It didn't click.

It was the next miracle of my new life: the mechanism closed, but I knew shackles well, and I was certain this one hadn't actually locked.

The Faceless slapped the second shackle over his own wrist, covering my inked name, and the lock clicked tight. He yanked the spider-chain and I stumbled forward.

"I refuse to live in a world perverted by mercy," he said. "As long as there's breath in my body, you will suffer every minute of your sentence. Now walk."

I had taken fewer than ten steps when a trumpeting blast rang out somewhere above the streets.

The elephant. It sounded close, very close. But how—?

The ground beneath us lurched. The Faceless nearly lost his footing. "What now?"

A second blow nearly knocked us both off our feet. A crack opened up in the pipe above us, and tiny shards of clay rained down.

The wall. The elephant had returned and had reached the wall. Being underground, we were feeling the aftershocks of the attack.

Bile rose to my throat. Zaraiyah had returned after all and re-started her assault. I'd left the barricade before seeing if she'd actually been captured. Evidently my Central friends had failed.

My friends—what had happened to them? Had the barricade fallen so swiftly?

From the impact, it seemed the monster had already done significant damage to the wall. How soon before it would start crushing buildings and killing innocents?

And here I was, helpless to do anything.

Kozi.

I reached for the sides of the pipe, hoping to brace myself for the next hit. The spider-chain grew taut as the Faceless pulled me forward.

The tunnel shook again, followed by a high-pitched screech of metal and the thud of something heavy falling. More thuds and metallic groans, and then ... nothing.

Eerie silence filled the space around us. For a moment I wondered if I'd lost my hearing. The tunnels had never been so quiet.

The hum of gears and the distant swish of water had ceased. Zaraiyah's monster had destroyed Tajim's Wheel.

The clay pipe beneath my feet vibrated, and in the distance I could make out an ominous hiss.

Oh no.

I darted toward a vertical shaft. The Faceless grabbed the spider-chain and yanked it, hard. "Where do you think you're—"

"Get out of the pipe!" I cried.

The hiss crescendoed in the tunnel ahead, growing to a roar. My captor pulled the chain again. "What trickery is this?"

"The tunnels are flooding—get to higher ground."

I lunged toward the vertical shaft at the top of the pipe, but my shackle pulled me back. Panicking, I grasped it with my other hand and yanked it hard—and it fell away.

With an adrenaline-fueled leap, I grabbed onto the lowest metal rung of the ladder. Swinging my now-free arm, I reached the next rung, hoisting myself up.

"Get down now or I'll shoot."

I glanced down and saw the Faceless, invisible in the darkness except for the gleam of the iron shackle around his wrist. The same chain I'd worn most of my life.

"Come with me." I lit my red fingertips and strained my arm toward him. "The water's already at your feet."

The black silhouette straightened. "As though need *your* help. I am my own light, and I can—"

A wall of black water smashed into him, cutting off his last words. The top of the surge caught my feet and nearly swept me off the ladder. I gripped the iron rungs as hard as I could and fought to pull my body higher into the vertical tunnel.

The water roared through the pipe beneath me, and I caught a glimpse of splintered timber and other wreckage from the docks.

My red lights flickered again, and I tried to take a steadying breath.

The sheer force of the water would have killed the Faceless instantly. At least he'd been spared the terror of drowning.

Swallowing back a wave of nausea, I ascended the next rung of the ladder.

A life of continual pain and endless striving, snuffed out in seconds. He'd worked so hard only to have everything cut off unfinished, unsatisfied.

Two weeks ago I would have regarded the death of an enemy with glee. Now with a heavy heart I wished his spirit peace, though somehow I doubted he would find it.

But there was no more time to reflect. The rush of water in the pipe below swirled up the shaft, and within seconds brackish water churned around my knees.

I scrambled up the slick rungs of the ladder toward the street-level grate, knowing that one slip and I'd be dead myself.

Now I reached the manhole cover, its lattice of daylight half-blinding me. I pushed against it to find this one not clay, but cold and metallic, too heavy for me to budge.

Trapped.

32

CRACK THE STONE

M ud-red water surged around my shoulders and rose over my head. I kicked and flailed, but its unrelenting force pinned me up against the metal.

I couldn't see, couldn't breathe, couldn't process the thought that I would die here, too.

And when I felt like I couldn't hold on a second longer, the water rose further still, lifting the manhole cover above me and tossing it aside as though it weighed nothing.

Spluttering, I kicked my way upward and managed to get my head above the surface.

Orange water sloshed through the city streets. Citizens stumbled through the waves around me, their arms filled with household goods and wailing children.

I struggled to my feet, the water at my knees threatening to knock me down again. A table floated by, followed by an overturned chair from an open doorway.

But the flooding was only a secondary worry. Over the sound of rushing water, another trumpet blast rang out. An ominous cloud of red dust rose from the direction of the river, and I could hear distant shouting.

I splashed my way toward the city's outer wall, trying to navigate the maze of muddy streets. Tall buildings obscured my view in every direction, making it impossible for me to tell where I was going.

A few minutes later, the imposing forty-foot height of the wall loomed ahead of me. But here its surface was fully intact.

I'd gotten turned around and arrived at the wrong part of town.

In the distance I could still hear shouts and the splintering of wood and metal. If only there were a way for me to see what was going on without risking getting lost again.

In this quiet part of the city, a building rose three stories, the back of the structure flush with the wall. I pushed aside the green curtain covering the doorway.

The room was empty besides a few lances propped in the corner and a mud-soaked cloak tossed over a table. A bright tapestry of geometrical shapes hung on one wall.

I recognized its olive green as the color the city guards wore. Apparently this was some sort of guard headquarters. I hoped it was abandoned because the guards were at the site of the attack and not hiding with the rest of B'jeme.

I pushed past the table toward the far wall. A stairway.

Taking the steps two at a time, I raced up all three stories until I came to the topmost room. Then I shimmied out the window, digging my claws into the mud siding. It crumbled beneath my claws, but I managed to swing myself onto the flat roof.

The top of the city wall still stretched another ten feet above me. I cursed softly and took a step back, peering at the cloud of rising dust. My ankle hit something wooden and I almost toppled back.

A wooden ladder lay flat on the rooftop. I heaved it up with some difficulty and propped it against the city wall. Exactly the right height.

Of course. If this was a guard-house, the city guards would need a way to see over the wall they were supposed to defend.

The wooden rungs creaked under my feet as I scaled the ladder and peered over the wall's ledge.

There. At the corner of the city, the elephant lifted a beam of wood with its trunk and smashed it into the wall. The shockwave nearly knocked me off the ladder.

Wood splinters rained onto the crushed dock below, and more dust rose as huge chunks of earth tumbled down.

The barricade at the monster's legs was completely smashed.

From here I could barely make out the small figures darting between the enormous white legs, throwing glass bottles and shaking jars of spices.

My friends.

The figures of the centaurs Egnatius and Castor—one pale, the other dark—led the charge, shouting unintelligible commands to the Central resistance force. But their daring efforts did nothing to slow the beast.

We were all so helpless.

Zaraiyah stood on the elephant's back, her powerful voice carrying easily over the din. She screamed at the monster, waving her blue scepter toward the ever-growing breach in the wall. With each movement, the elephant's head lurched forward. But the beast resisted, dead-set on its task.

I stepped higher on the ladder, my torso leaning precariously over the rounded top of the wall.

Now I could see the mangled metal and wooden remains of Tajim's Wheel. But the elephant didn't seem satisfied, lifting a heavy piston again and again with its trunk, trying to smash it against the splintering dock. Why was it so obsessed with the wheel?

It resents being replaced.

I caught my breath. What if this giant creature didn't just *look* like the old statue?

Old Folorunso had said the elephant statue—the one Makozi remembered—had been removed to make way for the wheel pump. The citizens had dumped it unceremoniously in the woods, where it had slowly languished and decayed.

What were the chances that Zaraiyah had brought a monster here that just happened to look like the bygone statue—color inaccuracies and all?

The old man had mused that she had a flair for poetic justice. But maybe she was simply resourceful.

I remembered back to my encounter with the creature at the barricade. I'd caught a huge whiff of magic as it drew close to me. Perhaps Zaraiyah had somehow channeled an enchantment powerful enough to animate the enormous statue left outside B'jeme's walls.

But how?

I watched again. Zaraiyah flicked her scepter, and the elephant's head moved at the same time. The lapis lazuli stone glowing on its forehead was identical to the jewel on the scepter's end.

The white elephant slammed the remaining shards of the iron piston into the water, capsizing a damaged dhow. The monster watched the boat sink and let out a satisfied snort.

At last the elephant turned toward the city wall, its heavy foot moving toward the breach.

"Aim for the jewel," I screamed towards my friends. But of course they were too far away to hear. Besides, their improvised weapons didn't have the accuracy needed to hit such a small target, especially not from the ground. It would take someone aiming from above to even have a chance.

An insane idea entered my head.

I glanced at the top of the city wall. Rain had taken its toll, smoothing away the edges and reducing the mud structure less than a foot wide. Walking along it would be suicide.

But with a good set of claws and enough desperation ...

No time to hesitate. I swung my right leg over the top of the mud wall, then my right arm. My head spun for a moment as I caught a glimpse of how small the barricade looked from up there.

Shutting my eyes, I lay my chest and stomach against the wall's surface, squeezing my knees on either side. The hard-packed mud was still slick from last night's rain.

I dug my claws in and pulled myself forward, inch by terrifying inch.

Within moments, mud coated my linen clothing, my arms, and even my face, making my whole body slippery.

I struggled to keep my eyes forward, but in my peripheral I could see the jumble of furniture and tent poles on the boardwalk almost forty feet below me.

A goblin could break her neck falling off of this.

My claws dug deeper into the mud, pulling myself toward the monster ahead. Something stiff pricked my thigh where it pressed against the wall. It took me a moment to figure it out: my obsidian shiv was still tucked away in my pocket, a remnant of the life I'd almost forgotten about. I managed to shift my weight so I wasn't leaning on it, counting myself lucky the blade hadn't sliced through the fabric and cut me.

Ahead, the elephant flapped its ears, then plunged its tusks into the wall. The red earth fell away in sheets, revealing huge logs that had reinforced the structure. They splintered and dangled unevenly throughout the wall, forming a treacherous ladder.

My world shuddered with the impact, and I lurched to one side, half-dangling over the barricade. With a grunt I pulled myself back to the top of the wall and fought my way forward. I couldn't give up now.

Besides, there was no survivable way down.

No time to worry about that, though. Another yard and I'd reach the crumbled end of the wall where the elephant rampaged.

The monster struck again, and cracks ran like lightning through the remaining wall, one fracture opening up in the mud beneath my hands.

Now or never.

I pulled myself as close to the crumbled ledge as I dared, shimmying my feet and hands to the wall's top surface. Perching on all fours, I tensed my body like a cat's. I dug my claws into the mud and flung myself forward, off the edge and toward the top of the elephant's head below.

For a second I sprawled, suspended in air, the only sensation the wind in my ears and the lurch of falling.

And then the beast jerked its head upward.

My knee smashed into the bony dome on the elephant's skull with a sickening snap. Immobilized by pain, I slid down the side of its giant face. At the last moment, someone threw me a white cloth and I grabbed it.

Only it wasn't a cloth. It was the elephant's white ear, big as a ship's sail. I plunged my claws in deep, leaving red lines in the white skin as gravity pulled me downward.

The elephant roared, and the world around me spun as it tossed its head and flapped its ears violently. All I could see were swirls of white and mud-red and cloud-grey.

The force slung me to the end of the ear, my grip weakening. An oddly calm part of my brain tried to analyze if I'd fly up into the sky or down into the wreckage below, and which would be worse.

Without warning, something grabbed me hard, forcing the air out of my lungs. Two huge, rubbery pincers wrapped around me —the end of the serpent-like trunk.

It slammed me onto the bony dome of the elephant's head, pinning me down with a crushing force. I couldn't breathe, and the pain radiating from my knee sent waves of nausea through me.

A pair of feet in beaded blue sandals walked toward me, then stomped on my green fingers viciously. "*You.*" Zaraiyah raised her scepter above me, the lapis lazuli glowing blue. The heavy trunk lifted away from my back, and I braced myself for a bone-crushing blow.

At that moment, between Zaraiyah's blue sandals, a muddy bare foot appeared. It kicked sideways, sweeping Zaraiyah's leg out from underneath her. As she fell, a small hand grabbed at the scepter, trying to wrestle it away from her grasp.

"Gangle?" How had the boy gotten up here? I thought of the treacherous jumble of logs and scrap metal and shuddered.

Gangle yanked at the scepter as Zaraiyah rose to her full height. The elephant's trunk swung wildly above me as the blue-robed woman and the raggedy boy fought over the staff that controlled it.

"Lady Hobgoblin, *go!*"

I tried to rise but my injured leg screamed in pain, and I found I couldn't move it, couldn't put weight on it. Laying on my stomach, I lowered myself down the elephant's face, desperately feeling for the stone somewhere between its eyes.

I heard Gangle laugh. "Yeah, you try to stop me, you fussy old peacock. Hey, *ow!*"

Something hot burned against my good leg, and I lowered myself further. The four-inch lapis lazuli glowed blue and seared my fingers as I grabbed it.

Ignoring the pain, I tried to yank the burning stone off the rough white skin, but the force that held it down was stronger than any adhesive I'd ever encountered.

"You're a disgusting urchin," Zaraiyah sneered somewhere above me.

Gangle laughed again. "Better an honest urchin than a selfish old—" An ominous thud cut off his words.

I couldn't wedge my claws underneath the stone, so I tried biting it off, ignoring the burns on my tongue and lips.

Suddenly a force jarred me so hard that it cracked one of my teeth, and nearly broke both my shoulders. The elephant's trunk rose into the air, poised to strike me again.

Zaraiyah had gotten hold of the scepter.

My desperation growing, I drew my obsidian shiv and jammed it into the blue gem. The black tip deflected off the stone, hardly scratching it. I raised my arm and stabbed at it again and again, my other hand clinging to the elephant's face for all it was worth.

Zaraiyah shouted to the elephant, and the trunk hurtled

toward me just as I stabbed the lapis lazuli with my remaining strength.

The blue stone cracked neatly down the middle.

My obsidian blade shattered in the process, one of the shards slicing deep into my palm.

Broken obsidian and the two halves of the jewel fell away toward the earth, and I felt myself slipping down with them. My legs could not cooperate, and my slick hands lost their grip.

I dug my claws into the elephant's skin, only to find it soft as chalk. Dry plaster crumbled into dust beneath my fingers, giving me nothing to hold onto.

I fell.

Above, I caught a glimpse of the white elephant, its head stiff and unmoving, the curled-back trunk frozen just inches from where I had been.

The red wall and the barricade blurred by and I plummeted straight for the water.

I heard the smack of my impact against the waves, but mercifully I never felt it.

33

FINAL BENEDICTION

M ist surrounded me, cold and grey.

My body felt as insubstantial as air, though if I concentrated hard enough, pain thrummed through my leg and hand. Undefined figures moved around me like shadows. I couldn't make out faces or guess at their shapes, and I wondered if they could see me.

In the corner of the room, some of the grey fog cleared. A woman in red stepped forward.

Fatima.

Golden circles and triangles danced over her long red dress, the colors more vibrant than any of Asuka's finest silks. The skin of her face was dark and smooth, her black curls cropped close to her scalp.

And this time, I could see her eyes, deep brown and intelligent. Makozi's eyes.

My heart caught in my throat. I wanted to tell her so many things—how her child was now safe, how he'd become dearer to me than my own life, how my heart broke for her, how I wished I'd had more time. But my mouth would not open, and my body would not move.

Fatima smiled, her eyes sad. She extended her dark hand toward me.

Ah.

Fatima was coming to escort me away.

So my injuries had been unsurvivable after all. I'd intended to fight with every ounce of strength in my body, and in the end, I had.

I still couldn't move, but I tried to communicate through my eyes that I was ready.

Fatima reached down and took my left hand in hers. The right one, I now noticed, was wrapped in bandages. When had that happened?

Her long, dark fingers wrapped around mine, and she didn't flinch at my claws or the blood-red fingertips. My hand rose in hers, though her touch felt as light as air.

I expected her to pull me to my feet, but she made no such effort. Instead, she gathered her red robe to the side, revealing a form I knew so well.

My little Makozi stood before me, tears brimming in his eyes. His body seemed brighter and more solid than Fatima's and mine, and the grey mist pulled away from him.

The woman in red paused, a tear running down her dark face, and placed a kiss on his forehead.

Makozi didn't even flinch.

Fatima nudged the boy toward me. She bowed her head and placed Makozi's hand in mine. His fingers were solid and warm and had that whiff of humanity I now loved.

I gathered just enough strength to squeeze my fingers around his. I looked once again toward Fatima, but she was gone, and the mist was gone, and I lay on a cot with Makozi by my side.

"Doctor Jolinea, look," said a familiar voice. I lay in the little houseboat once more, and Asuka leaned over me eagerly.

The Rikean doctor placed a cool cloth over my forehead. "Good to see you awake. Don't try to get up—rest."

I managed to form words. "I dying?"

"No, Magma. You've been badly injured. The damage to your knee is especially concerning—you may never get full use back. But nothing is fatal. You're going to live."

Makozi tugged on the doctor's white robe. "She's all better?"

"She will be soon, little one. Especially with you beside her."

I reached out and stroked Makozi's curls. My fingers brushed his forehead and I felt a tingle where Fatima had kissed him.

His mother's final benediction. I squeezed my eyes closed, too overcome to speak.

A moment later a hand touched my shoulder. Asuka held out a bowl of soup.

I turned my head away, still too disoriented to eat yet. My lips formed the question I wasn't sure I wanted to ask.

"... Etsuko?"

"Magma-sama." Asuka's voice swelled with gratitude. "Etsuko lives, Magma-sama. Mareso sits beside her healing-bed in the city, and sends news of her improvement. My Etsuko lives because of you."

"And Gangle?"

"Safe, too." She chuckled. "They're calling him a hero. The only danger he's in now is from a head swollen with pride. His uncle in the city will have his hands full."

"Oh, Magma, there's good news," Makozi said. "Someone put our relevant back. Show her, Asuka-san."

Asuka pulled back a curtain and propped me up on my cot.

I squinted in the red-orange light—I'd made it to another sunset, after all—and it took my eyes a moment to adjust. There, by the crumbled corner of the city, a plaster elephant stood, its trunk curled like a serpent, one foot raised. Red handprints were smeared down one side of its face.

My handprints, my blood.

"Zaraiyah has been captured and is on her way to Alavar," the doctor said. "We'll see what punishment Selena and the Council deem worthy."

My eyes moved from the plaster elephant to what remained of

the barricade. Vindor's Central Market had been destroyed, and with it the livelihoods of hundreds. Olayo and Zaraiyah's childish feud had caused so much suffering for innocent people.

As I watched, a stream of B'jeme citizens climbed down the stairs from the now-opened gate, surveying the destruction. A snatch of conversation floated through the houseboat's window.

"Was this your pottery?" an old man asked.

"Yes," came a dejected voice. "The finest Shido had to offer."

"And how much would each of these have sold for?"

"One hundred gold coins. One-fifty on a good day. And I had six."

"Izoma," the old man's voice called. "Run home and fetch the money from under the bed. For you, brave patriot of the Barricade, I'll pay for the lot."

"Oh," a woman said. "Take my bracelet. It's turquoise. I trust this will be enough to rebuild your booth."

It was a pattern I would soon become familiar with—citizens of B'jeme, who days ago had clutched their coins in fear, now poured them out for the Centrals who'd defended their city.

"Magma." Makozi still clutched my hand. "Why are you so sick? I want you to get up."

I kissed his curly head, inhaling his human scent. "Not yet, Kozi. But soon."

"I very love you, Magma."

"And I very love you, Kozi. More than anybody. Forever and ever."

"And you're going to stay?"

I stopped. With the Faceless gone, could I ...?

"Yes, Makozi," Asuka said. "Magma-sama is going to stay here, with me." She held up her hand at the start of my protest. "I won't hear of it. You have saved my only child. From now on my food, my home, my goods—everything I have I will share with you."

"I'm afraid that's not possible." Mistress Innosa stepped into the houseboat, her crisp, black robe looking out of place among the scratched and dented floorboards. "Do you realize that Magma is a fugitive of the law?"

Confusion clouded Asuka's face. "How could Magma-sama be guilty of a crime?"

I looked away.

"Well, she's wanted by her native government," Mistress Innosa said. "And as such, she's in constant danger of re-capture."

Of course she was right. The Dominion always had its ways.

"The good news," said Mistress Innosa, "is that Vindorian international law gives political fugitives sanctuary within certain locations." The regal woman turned to me. "Magma, this is what I tried to tell you earlier. The House of Mercy, as a worship center, is a place of sanctuary. As long as you are within our walls, no one can take you away."

"You mean—" My voice became a whisper. "I can stay with Kozi?"

"We insist on it," Mistress Innosa said firmly. "The teachers and I have all pooled together our savings to purchase you and the boy permanent stamps. You may stay as long as you wish. Folorunso, for the record, is very eager to hire an assistant gardener." She winked. "He's getting lazy in his old age, after all."

"Magma's staying?" Makozi's eyes shone.

"Yes." I pulled him into an embrace. "Magma stays with Kozi forever."

"And then Mama will come, and we'll all be three together."

A lump rose in my throat, and I squeezed his hand. "Ah. Magma and Kozi will talk about that tomorrow."

THE REST of the city's history, of course, is well documented. The breached portion of the wall was eventually rebuilt and flooding damage was repaired, though you can still see the waterline on some of the buildings.

Tajim's Second Wheel was reconstructed closer to the gate. The elephant got to keep its hard-won corner, and its plaster is

regularly re-applied to keep it from falling apart again. It's funny
how the people look so kindly on this eyesore despite its destruc-
tive history.

Or maybe it's because of it.

My handprints are long gone, of course, but the blood-red
flag the citizens have added to the elephant monument reminds us
of the Centrals of the Barricade.

Today the city gate is always open to our Central friends, as
are our homes and our hearts. The citizens of B'jeme are
renowned throughout Vindor for our generosity to those in need,
eager hospitality to strangers, and genuine love for the foreigners
among us.

And when you measure wealth this way, and not in the
number of coins clutched in your fist, we are truly the richest
people in all Vindor.

I, of course, have lived at the House of Mercy since my recov-
ery, in a small room I share with Makozi. On a single shelf we keep
our two most treasured items—the Bandit King's mug, and a
well-loved doll with short black hair and a red dress. Sometimes I
hear Makozi whispering to her, telling her the things closest to his
heart, just as he did when he was five.

Mistress Innosa makes a point of stopping by every evening,
as though we need more doting on. Her kindness has been never-
failing. But her greatest gift has been teaching me this: that the
compassion of the Bandit King was merely a shadow of the
greatest mercy of all.

Each night, I hobble out into the starlit gardens that Old
Folorunso and I have built together, and through the mystery of
roots and soil I make a life for myself and my son. A few flowers at
my feet and above me the stars—what more can I ask?

During the heat of the day, I sleep while Makozi studies. I
wake each afternoon to the sound of a slamming door (he can't
not slam the door) and I rise to his chatter and laughter.

He towers above me now, like all other humans of his age, and his brown eyes sparkle when he speaks of donning the green of the city guards next year.

"Maybe I'll join the guards, too," I tell him. "I know a thing or three about defending B'jeme."

Perhaps one day I'll make the journey back to Ipktu. But I have a long-standing promise never to leave Makozi behind, and I'm not ready to bring him on that trek yet.

I feel that the Bandit King, if he knew, would understand. For while the Bandit King released me from the darkness within my soul, it was Makozi who lit my heart bright with love. And it was his love that opened up the world to me.

Left to myself, I'd still be running and hiding in caves, blind to the beauty of the stars and sunsets. I'd never have found home: this place with my son, in this community of people—citizens and Centrals alike—that I count as my dearest friends.

Such is the power of love. It's that small, trivial thing that the powerful sneer at and the selfish keep at bay. But allowed its course it will topple evil, transform cities, melt stone hearts, and bring the dead—like me—back to life.

No water can quench love, and no river can sweep it away. For does not the universe itself run on Love?

"Love is the foolishness of men, and the wisdom of God."

—Victor Hugo, *Les Misérables*

Don't miss the next installment of ...

A CLASSIC RETOLD

STEAL THE MORROW
Jenelle Leanne Schmidt

The city may be dangerous, but it holds his only hope...

Abandoned on a remote highway after bandits murder his parents, young Olifur finds safety with Fritjof. The gruff woodsman teaches him and other orphans to live off the land. When Fritjof falls ill, Olifur will risk everything to save his mentor —even travel to far-off Melar seeking a doctor.

However, the city of Melar is more perilous than Olifur imagined, and doctors aren't cheap. His quest leads him first to a hazardous job working on the elevated trains high above the city. But the dangers in the clouds are nothing compared to those on the ground. Olifur soon finds himself ensnared in a web of professional thieves, and he must think fast if he is to survive the day and bring the much-needed aid to Fritjof before it is too late.

Schmidt reweaves Charles Dickens' "Oliver Twist" into an exciting tale of integrity and perseverance in this gaslamp-fantasy adventure.

ACKNOWLEDGMENTS

When I wrote *Escape to Vindor* and *Mists of Paracosmia*, I was a different person. It was after I completed both drafts of the duology that my sons came into my life. *Crack the Stone* is my first motherhood story, an exploration of this insane-but-amazing journey I've only just begun.

David and Jonathan, when you're old enough to read this, know that your mom very, very loves you, all the days ever. (And David, thank you for all the funny "Davidisms" that directly inspired Makozi's speech.)

To my own mother, Dr. Margaret Park, who raised four girls on her own amidst difficult circumstances: Before I was a parent, I admired your strength. Now that I'm a mother myself, I'm astounded by it. Thank you for your tenacious love. And to Rob and Pat Golus: thank you for being the best second set of parents anyone could ask for. I'm so glad to be part of your family.

To my true love, Mike Golus: My motherhood journey had a rocky start, and your dedication, kindness, and hard work have kept me sane. Thank you also for the myriad ways you support my writing dream. Dear readers, wait for the right one, no matter how long it takes.

To Allison Tebo, who invited me into this wonderful project: Thank you for all you've done to make this dream happen, and for helping me get my writing mojo back. To Jenelle Leanne Schmidt, Hannah Kaye, Rosie Grymm, Alissa J. Zavalianos, Emily Hayse, Nina Clare, and Tor Thibeaux: I'm honored to be named among you. Your fellowship, along with that of Penny Kearney, has encouraged me more than you know.

Thanks also go to Emily Newman, for your insights on adoption and trauma healing; to AnjolaOluwa, for your help navigating West African culture, particularly in regards to Yoruba and Igbo names; and to Mary Denmen, for your editing expertise and for making sure my characters use their indoor voices instead of suddenly! Shouting! Excitedly! All the time!

Finally, to Jesus Christ, whose mercy and grace revolutionized my life: I was cold and self-righteous and on track to be the Faceless. You brought me back from the dead; You rescued me from myself; You softened my stone heart into Magma.

Emily Golus

SPECIAL THANKS GO TO THE FOLLOWING READERS:

Defenders of B'jeme

Vanessa Anderson	Jessica Flory	Emily Newman
Bekki Beilby	Kendra Graham	Molly Park
Beth Cunningham	Olivia Gratehouse	D.T. Powell
Julianna Dotson	Karen Guthrie	Jillian Sevilla-Sales
Reagan Dotson	Anna Lisa Haskell	Ruth Steel
Erin Dydek	Shannon Hugo	Emma Stephens
Sarah Efird	Sarah LaCourse	Shannon Stewart
Barbara V. Evers	Jess Lindsey	Karen Tyner
	Sierra Lyon	

The Council of Vindor

Arions
Emily Newman
Sarah LaCourse

Dembeyans
Reagan Dotson

Fairy Folk
Leah Smit
Emma Stephens

Huntsmen
Janice Robinson
Shannon Stewart

Ipktu Goblins
Allison Tebo
D.T. Powell
Shannon Hugo
Mary Herceg

Kavannans
Karen Guthrie

Loray
Julianna Dotson
Jillian Sevilla-Sales

Mauritians
Erin Dydek

Rikeans
Judith DeStefano

Selks
Jess Lindsey

ABOUT THE AUTHOR

Emily Golus is an award-winning fantasy author with nearly 20 years of professional writing experience. She is the author of *Escape to Vindor*, which won the 2017 Selah Award for Young Adult Fiction, and *Mists of Paracosmia*. Golus aims to engage, inspire, and show how small acts of courage and love can create meaningful change.

Golus lives in Greenville, SC with her husband, Mike, who is her greatest supporter. They have two active little boys and enjoy hiking, making Thai food, and exploring small towns in the Carolinas.

Learn more about the many nations featured in *Crack the Stone* at WorldofVindor.com, and keep up with book news at EmilyGolusBooks.com.

Printed in the USA
CPSIA information can be obtained
at www.ICGtesting.com
LVHW090255310823
756768LV00003B/14